Purrs and Peril – A
Norwegian Forest Cat Café
Cozy Mystery – Book 1

by

Jinty James

Purrs and Peril – A Norwegian Forest Cat Café Cozy Mystery – Book 1

by

Jinty James

Copyright © 2018 by Jinty James

All rights reserved

No part of this publication may be copied, reproduced in any format, by any means, electronic or otherwise, without prior consent from the copyright owner and publisher of this book.

This is a work of fiction. All characters, names, places and events are the product of the author's imagination or used fictitiously.

First paperback edition April 2019

CHAPTER 1

"What do you think, Annie?" Lauren Crenshaw bent down to her fluffy silver-gray tabby, aware of the soft buzz of conversation filling the coffee shop that morning.

"Brrt." The three-year-old Norwegian Forest cat, for whom the Norwegian Forest Café had been named, sounded happy as she gazed at the customers seated in the welcoming cocoon created by pale yellow walls and pine tables and chairs. Although it was a certified cat café, Annie was the only cat on the premises, and sometimes seemed to think it was *her* café, not hers and Lauren's.

The scent of freshly ground coffee, good butter, and sweet cinnamon delighted Lauren's senses and filled her with a sense of contentment.

A few months ago, she'd inherited her grandmother's café and adjoining Victorian cottage in picturesque Gold Leaf Valley, northern California. Dating from the 1800s gold rush, the small town boasted charming Victorian houses and a friendly community.

She'd been close to her grandmother and had often visited her on the weekends, accompanied by Annie. When she discovered Gramms had left her the business and house, Lauren decided in a split second to leave her boring office job in Sacramento and plunge into the world of running a café.

It wasn't as if she hadn't had help, though. She'd also inherited Gramm's employee Ed, a fifty-something part-time baker who made pastry like a dream. He was big and burly, and grunted rather than talked. But when customers lined up to buy his croissants and Danishes, Lauren knew she had to keep him on.

She didn't know how her grandmother had run the coffee shop with Ed as her only employee, although Lauren had helped out when she'd visited. The woman had been a dynamo until eighty, when old-age started to slow her down. She had died peacefully in her sleep, a loss that Lauren – and Annie – were still coming to terms with.

"Hey, boss, Annie's got some new customers." Her second cousin Zoe Crenshaw zipped up to them, wearing jeans and a hot-pink t-shirt. Five foot seven with a brunette pixie cut that highlighted her cute features and sparkling brown eyes, she was a live-wire.

In contrast, Lauren was one inch shorter, a little curvy, with a dusting of freckles on her nose, light brown hair with hints of gold ending at just below her chin, and hazel eyes. Her usual work outfit consisted of pale blue capris and t-shirts in soft muted colors, like peach and apricot.

"Brrt!" Annie's green eyes lit up at the sight of two middle-aged women hovering at the *Please Wait to Be Seated* sign. She sauntered over to the ladies, tilting her head in a way that said, "Follow me."

"Well," one of the women said uncertainly, "Glenda told us it *was* a cat café."

Annie stopped and pivoted, as if encouraging them to follow her, before leading them to an empty table in the corner.

"Annie will find the best table for you," Lauren called out to the ladies, giving them an encouraging smile.

They smiled back, following the silver tabby, and seating themselves at the table she'd chosen for them.

"They'll be raving fans by the time they leave here," Zoe predicted. "Especially with Ed making apricot Danish today."

"Don't remind me," Lauren said ruefully. She'd treated herself to one of the buttery, flaky, melt-in-your-mouth pastries that morning, and was still fighting herself on going back for a second serving.

Perhaps that was why she would never be a skinny twig. But surely rushing around the café all day burned off extra calories? It was a theory that needed more testing, she told herself. After all, she'd only been running the café for the last three months.

"I'd better bus that table." Zoe gestured to the table to the right. The customers had just departed, leaving what looked like a sizeable tip.

"I'll help you." Lauren had no idea if she'd be able to run the café without her cousin helping out like a butterfly buzzing with caffeine. Zoe had visited one weekend after Lauren had just re-opened the café, waving away Lauren's attempt to pay her. The cousins had always looked forward to seeing each other at family get togethers, but since Zoe lived in San Francisco hopping from one temp job to another, and Lauren had lived in Sacramento, the two of them getting together for a regular catch-up had been a bit problematic.

That weekend, Lauren had impulsively offered Zoe a full-time job at the café, and her cousin had jumped at the offer. Now they shared Lauren's cottage (luckily it had two bedrooms) and often explored the small town together on their days off.

"Ten dollars!" Zoe placed the tip left on the table in her pocket. "I'll put it in the tip jar."

"Thanks." Lauren smiled. Zoe and Ed the baker shared the tips, Lauren and Zoe reasoning that if Ed didn't make his feather-light pastries, the tips wouldn't be nearly as forthcoming. Since Lauren owned the café and made a small profit as well as a wage, she didn't think it fair to take a share of the gratuities.

Lauren could bake – but pastry was a bit of a mystery to her. She could make it if she had to, but she was the first to admit that her attempts weren't nearly as good as Ed's.

But she was great at making cakes and cupcakes. Perhaps that was part of the problem. Although she was critical of her baking, she was the first to admit if she had made a particularly delicious cake. And she would only know if it was delicious if she *tested* it.

"Brrt?" Annie trotted toward the front door, her gray ears pricked. A man of medium height and in his forties smiled wearily at the feline.

"I just need some coffee to go today, Annie," he said.

"Brrp." Annie seemed to nod, and then led the way to the counter.

Croissants with the perfect ratio of buttery flakey goodness, plump apricot halves brushed with a touch of sweet glaze and glistening with temptation nestled on top of light, Danish pastry in the glass case. Next to them were several varieties of cupcakes, such as chocolate, and raspberry swirl, finished with tempting swirls of frosting.

"I'd better go and make Steve's coffee," Lauren told Zoe, and hurried over to the counter.

"I need a large latte today, Lauren." Steve dug out his wallet from his pants' pocket.

"Everything okay?" Lauren began steaming the milk, watching Annie make her way to her pink bed on the corner shelf. It was high enough to give her privacy from the customers if she needed it, but easy for her to jump into.

"It probably will be." Strained lines bracketed his face. His short sandy hair receded at his temples, and tiny pinch marks on his nose indicated that he'd worn his reading glasses recently.

"You're not working too hard, are you?" she asked, pouring three shots of espresso into a big cardboard cup. Steve was a coffee fiend and she knew he could handle that much coffee at once.

"I am at the moment." He grimaced. "But hopefully things will sort themselves out."

"I'll keep my fingers crossed." She gazed at him in concern. Steve usually came in every day for a latte, but she'd never seen him look like this. Although, now she thought about it, he had seemed anxious last week.

"You haven't got too many clients on at the moment?" she asked delicately, not wanting to sound nosy.

"No." He shook his head. "Just one accountancy job at the moment – thank goodness. It hasn't exactly turned out the way I expected."

"You're auditing the church's accounts, aren't you?" She handed him his coffee.

"Yes." He took a sip of his latte, his eyes closing for a second. "But I can't say anything more about it."

"I understand." Was it her imagination or did he look a little better after tasting the strong coffee? "When you're not busy, I'd love to hire you to look over my accounts."

He smiled. "Hopefully in a couple of weeks I'll be free."

"Great. Just let me know."

Steve waved goodbye to her, and Annie sitting in her cat bed, before departing.

Before Lauren could wonder any more about why Steve looked so worried, her attention was taken up with an influx of new customers, oohing and ahhing when they spotted Annie.

The day sped by. She only realized it was mid-afternoon when Pamela, a regular customer who always dressed smartly, walked in, accompanied by two of her friends. The three middle-aged ladies stood inside the entrance, waiting to be seated.

Lauren was just about to call Annie, when the silver tabby spotted the new customers and made a beeline for them.

"Brrt," she said importantly, leading the way to a four-seater table in the middle of the café.

Lauren had kept an eye on the Norwegian Forest Cat all day, making sure she didn't get too overwhelmed with the constant stream of customers.

When she and Annie had moved in to her grandmother's cottage, which connected to the café via a private hallway, Lauren had installed a cat flap in the cottage door, and one in the shop door. Annie could go home whenever she liked – but she usually stayed in the café until Lauren closed around five o'clock.

Now, Lauren smiled at Annie's choice of table. Pamela seemed to like being the center of attention, and holding court at the café. Most customers ordered at the counter – the suggestion was printed on the menu – but Pamela appeared to expect table service.

"What can I get you?" Lauren headed over to the trio, whipping out the notepad and pencil she kept in the pocket of her capris.

"Hmm." Pamela tapped the laminated menu, her long, blonde bob swinging forward. "It says the cakes are displayed in the counter. What sort of cakes do you have?"

Since Lauren knew from experience that Pamela was not inclined to walk over there herself to inspect the sweet treats, she answered patiently. "Croissants, apricot Danish, chocolate cupcakes, and raspberry swirl cupcakes."

"Ooh, raspberry swirl!" One of Pamela's companions clapped a hand to her mouth, as if realizing she'd spoken out of turn.

"You don't have anything else?" Pamela queried. "I was in the mood for a slice of lemon poppyseed cake."

"We don't have any today," Lauren replied. "All our cakes and pastries are freshly baked, so we only make what we think will sell that day."

"Quite right." A stout middle-aged woman sat on Pamela's other side. "All this food waste is terrible. Glad you're trying to do the right thing."

"Thank you." Lauren smiled at the woman. She hadn't seen her in the café before. Hopefully, if she enjoyed her visit today, she would become a new customer.

"I suppose I'll have a chocolate cupcake." Pamela sighed, as if it was just *too* terrible there wasn't much else to choose from. "And a vanilla almond latte – you *do* have almond milk, don't you?"

Yes, we do," Lauren replied, the same answer she'd given Pamela last week when she'd asked for the same drink.

"I'll have an apricot Danish," the stout woman said. "My friends have been telling me about them. And a pot of tea." She frowned. "You do have tea, don't you? English Breakfast?"

"Yes," Lauren answered, knowing that very item was printed on the menu on the table. Perhaps the woman had left her reading glasses at home.

"I'll have a latte please," the raspberry swirl woman spoke.

"Thank you, ladies." Lauren hurried to the counter, already wondering if Pamela would leave a tip. Probably not, judging by past visits. Oh, well. She made a decent profit on coffee and tea, as well as the baked goods. And someone had recommended Ed's apricot Danish!

Lauren returned to the table with their order, noticing that Pamela sounded very pleased with herself. "And I said to him, "My dear, I may not live in Sacramento, but I am not a complete savage!"

The other ladies giggled.

"Gold Leaf Valley is far superior to Sacramento, if you ask me," the stout lady opined. "We've got everything we need right here."

"Oh, yes," the raspberry swirl lady said. "A just big enough supermarket, some nice restaurants, and this wonderful coffee shop." She gazed around the room, her face lighting up as she spotted Annie sitting in her cat bed. "Your cat is just wonderful, dear." She patted Lauren's arm.

"Thank you," Lauren replied as she pulled off the check from her notepad and placed it on the table.

"We're paying separately Lauren, *if* you didn't realize," Pamela said.

Lauren groaned inwardly. *Of course* they would be. She should have assumed that from the start – especially with Pamela.

"No problem." She forced a smile as she quickly wrote three bills. She was excellent at simple math. It was advanced algebra and physics she'd always had problems with in school.

"Here you go." She placed each bill in front of the appropriate customer.

"Thank you." The stout woman nodded.

Lauren flashed a genuine smile, and hurried back to the counter. Where was Zoe? In situations like this, she appreciated a wing woman.

"Oops!" Zoe burst through the swinging kitchen doors and skidded to a stop beside Lauren. "Too late to help with you know who." She nodded at Pamela's table.

"How did you know she was here?"

"Ed told me. He must have seen her when he checked how many customers we had. You know he likes to leave by four."

"Yes." Lauren was grateful he worked 'til then. He could have easily left by lunchtime, when his pastries had all been baked, cooled and placed in the glass display cases. Instead, when she'd taken over, he'd stated he would work the same hours he had for her grandmother, who'd closed the café around four o'clock.

"Annie!" A sweet voice quavered. "Will you take me to my table, darling?"

Annie jumped down from her cat bed and trotted to the old lady standing in the doorway, leaning on a walking stick. Her gray hair was piled on top her head in a bun, and she wore a beige skirt with a dusty rose cardigan which seemed just right for the April weather.

"Mrs. Finch," Lauren and Zoe chorused softly.

The senior was a favorite of theirs, who seemed to appreciate everything she ordered and always left a tip. Lauren suspected she was one of Annie's favorites, as well.

Annie walked by Mrs. Finch's side, matching her pace, as if she knew not to hurry the elderly customer.

Lauren waited until Mrs. Finch was seated, then made her way to the small table Annie had chosen for the senior. It was tucked in an alcove, out of the way of the bustle, but from this vantage point, Mrs. Finch would have a good view of the rest of the cafe. Annie perched on the opposite chair.

"I must say hi to her," Zoe murmured as she joined Lauren.

"Hello, girls," Mrs. Finch greeted them.

"Hello," Lauren replied, smiling.

"Hi, Mrs. Finch!" Zoe said.

"What can we get you?" Lauren fished out her notepad and pencil.

"Whatever you think is best," Mrs. Finch said. "Annie, what do you think I should have?"

"Brrt!"

"I think she means everything is good," Zoe said with a giggle.

"How about a raspberry swirl cupcake and a pot of tea?" Lauren suggested.

"That sounds wonderful," Mrs. Finch slowly relaxed in the chair.

"Is something wrong, Mrs. Finch?" Zoe crinkled her brow as she studied the senior.

"It's my garden." She sighed. "A small branch from my oak tree came down in the wind last night and there are leaves everywhere. I had a good look at the mess this morning, and now some other plants look a little different in some way." She frowned. "I haven't been out in the garden for a few days and now I just can't put my finger on what's wrong." She shook her head, causing a strand of hair to fall out of her bun.

"Maybe it's just extra damage from the wind," Zoe suggested.

"I suppose that must be it." The senior smiled ruefully. "Can you recommend anyone who could tidy up my garden for me? Teenagers, perhaps, who need extra spending money? Usually my neighbor Steve helps me out but he's busy with his accounting business at the moment."

"Maybe Pastor Mike would know," Lauren suggested. The local preacher ran a youth ministry, and was a regular customer.

"Oh, that is a good idea." Mrs. Finch's expression brightened. "And I have his number at home. I'll call him later today."

"Awesome!" Zoe grinned.

"Let us know if we can do anything else to help," Lauren said. Mrs. Finch was eighty-two and lived alone in a house in the next block. She walked to the café on her own just about every day. Lauren just hoped she would be as spry at that age.

Annie stayed at the table when Lauren and Zoe departed.

"Poor Mrs. Finch," Zoe whispered as they headed to the counter. "Do you really think something is different in her garden, or do you think she's imagined something again?"

"I don't know." Lauren got out a white teapot and spooned loose leaf tea into it. "Last month she was sure she'd lost two library books, and we found them on the table on her front porch – she'd forgotten to take them to the library. But if she can't tell for sure that something's wrong in her garden, then maybe it was just wind damage making a mess, like she said."

"I could hear the magnolia tapping on my bedroom window last night. That wind was fierce." Zoe shivered. "I was glad I wasn't living alone."

"I nearly knocked on your door last night, asking if you'd like some hot chocolate – and company. But I didn't want you to think I was a baby." Lauren smiled ruefully.

Zoe grinned. "Let's make a pact that if one of us is scared about anything, we'll tell the other right away."

"Deal." The cousins high-fived each other.

"Did the wind bother Annie?" Zoe asked as she put a cupcake on a white china plate.

"No. She was fast asleep on my bed. I told myself if my cat wasn't scared of the weather, then I shouldn't be, either."

Lauren took the tray over to Mrs. Finch, interrupting her conversation with Annie. She was telling the feline about her trip to the grocery store yesterday.

"I hope you enjoy this, Mrs. Finch." Lauren placed the cupcake and teapot in front of her. "Would you like me to pour?"

"If you would, dear. My hands aren't as steady as they used to be."

Lauren poured the tea and added the milk, knowing the old lady enjoyed a dash. She made sure not to fill the cup up to the top, so if Mrs. Finch's hand was unsteady, she wouldn't spill the hot liquid on herself – hopefully.

"Call me if you'd like anything else," Lauren glanced at the Norwegian Forest Cat. "Or send Annie to get me."

"Brrt," Annie replied importantly.

"I will, dear." Mrs. Finch smiled. Lauren noticed her pink lipstick was a little smudged. "I must say, you've done a wonderful job here. I used to come all the time when your dear grandmother was alive, you know. And it's just as good—" she glanced at Annie "—if not better now."

"Thank you," Lauren replied, glad that one of her favorite customers was happy with the café's new incarnation.

Lauren noticed a customer waiting at the counter and hurried over to serve him. Zoe must be in the kitchen, doing the dishes. They had a dishwasher, but sometimes it was quicker to wash the crockery as and when needed during the day.

"I'm going." Ed pushed open the swinging door. Big and burly, he had monster rolling pins for arms, full of muscle.

"Thanks, Ed." Lauren smiled.

"I won't be in tomorrow," he warned. "Dental appointment."

"I know. I'll make extra cupcakes."

"Good," he grunted, and returned to the kitchen.

"The dishes are up to date," Zoe declared a few minutes later as she emerged from the kitchen. "And Ed's gone home."

"I know." Lauren nodded.

"Do you think I could leave a couple of minutes early today?" Zoe checked her watch.

"Sure."

"Thanks."

Lauren hesitated. "Are you going to tell me why?" She wasn't nosy, just curious, she told herself. Besides, her cousin usually told her everything about her life – even if sometimes it was a little bit TMI.

"I've got a date!" Zoe looked like she wanted to jump up and down.

"Another one?" Lauren inwardly groaned.

"That's why I didn't tell you." Zoe bit her lip. "But I've got a good feeling about this one, I swear."

"That's what you said last time," Lauren reminded her. "And he left you stuck in a Japanese restaurant in Sacramento, with the bill."

"I know." Zoe looked downcast for a moment. "Which is why—" her naturally sunny personality re-emerged "—we're meeting at a local restaurant this time. And, I'm going to ask the server for separate checks from the start. So if he does try to stick me with the bill, it won't work!"

"Who is he?" Lauren asked. Her cousin had been internet dating for a few months now, bemoaning the lack of eligible men in Gold Leaf Valley – unless you wanted a boyfriend over the age of forty. Lauren continually reminded her that wasn't *quite* true.

"He's five foot ten, so a little taller than me," Zoe replied. "And he has a job!"

"That's encouraging," Lauren said, wondering if her generation should be so easily pleased.

"And he lives in Marysville but he said he likes Gold Leaf Valley, so it's no problem to meet me here for dinner."

"Good. What time are you meeting him?"

"Seven. But I want to have a shower and decide what to wear. And then walk over to the steakhouse."

"I'll drive you," Lauren offered. Zoe didn't own a car. She hadn't needed one in San Francisco. "In fact, why don't you borrow my car again? That way you'll be able to come home whenever you like."

"Are you sure?"

"Of course. I want you to be safe." Lauren didn't have any plans for the evening apart from watching something on Netflix with Annie. "Do you want me to call you at 7.30 and see how you're doing? I could be your emergency phone call."

"I want to be totally optimistic and say that won't be necessary but after the Japanese restaurant incident, I think it's a good idea." Zoe sighed. "I know you think I'm wasting my time dating like this, but I would like to get married one day – whenever that will be."

"I know. So do I." Lauren couldn't help wondering what was wrong with meeting a potential love interest the old-fashioned way – in person first. But she had to admit, however reluctantly, that that wasn't working out for her at the moment – and hadn't for a while.

"Hey, if tonight is a success, maybe he's got a brother or a friend you could meet – like a blind date!" Zoe laughed. "Just like dating last century!"

"I'm not ready for orthopedic shoes yet – I'm only twenty-six!" Lauren protested. She was one year older than Zoe.

"That's what you say," her cousin teased.

"Brrp!" Annie trotted to the counter.

"Is Mrs. Finch okay?" Lauren asked.

"Brrt." Annie seemed to nod her head.

"Maybe she's ready to pay," Zoe suggested.

"I'll go check." Lauren walked over to the secluded table, Annie by her side.

"It was lovely, Lauren." Mrs. Finch pulled her tan wallet out of her handbag, her hand trembling. "Here you go." She pressed the money into Lauren's hand, along with the bill. "Buy a little something for Annie."

"Thank you. I will." Lauren smiled. "Would you like Zoe to walk you home? It's no bother."

"I'll be fine." Mrs. Finch managed to stand without much trouble. "It's not far to my house."

"If you're sure?"

"Annie could escort me through to the door."

"Brrp." Annie walked slowly toward the entrance, looking over her shoulder as if checking Mrs. Finch followed.

Lauren watched the two of them make their way to the front door.

"Mrs. Finch looks like she'll be okay," Zoe observed.

"I hope so," Lauren replied, wondering if Annie was intuitive enough to tell her if she thought Mrs. Finch wasn't up to walking home by herself. Probably.

"If you don't need me, I'm going to get ready for my date." Zoe's eyes sparkled. "Don't wait up!"

CHAPTER 2

Zoe gulped down her latte the next morning. They were due to open the café in a few minutes. Annie sat opposite, looking bright-eyed and interested, her long whiskers shining in the sunlight.

"It was a disaster," Zoe moaned. "He didn't look like his photo – at all. That picture must have been taken when he was twenty or something. His profile said he was thirty-seven—" she raised a hand "—I know, a bit old but I thought, hey, he's under forty. Nuh-uh." She shook her head.

"Oh." Lauren's heart went out to her cousin. She hadn't heard anything about Zoe's date last night, not even when her cousin had returned home at nine o'clock. She'd muttered, "I'll tell you about it tomorrow," and escaped to her bedroom.

"He must have been forty-five – maybe older!" Zoe sounded outraged.

"But when I called at 7.30 you sounded okay," Lauren said.

"I know. He was a few minutes late, and yes, I was totally disappointed with his appearance, but I thought, Lauren would say to give him a chance. Maybe he isn't as old as he looks. And he did seem to be five foot ten, so his profile wasn't a complete lie."

"So what happened?" Lauren leaned forward. So did Annie.

"We asked for separate checks, so that bit was okay," Zoe continued. "But I think he's a cheapskate. He actually suggested we go back to my place for dessert to save money!"

"He didn't!"

"Yep." Zoe nodded. "There's no way I'm going to invite a first date back to my – your – place. Not these days. Not even in Gold Leaf Valley. So I told him, sure. But I should call my roommate and ask her if she can put Rudy, her Rottweiler, out on the porch. Because Rudy's used to being inside the house at night to protect us. You should have seen him pale." Zoe laughed.

Lauren joined in with a giggle.

"Then he looked at his watch and said never mind, he had to get up for work early, anyway. He called the server over, paid his check and left."

"I haven't heard you use that excuse before. I think you should use it all the time from now on."

"You bet I will!" Zoe blew back a lock of hair that brushed her face. Her pixie cut was short, apart from a few strands that substituted for bangs covering her forehead.

"Was that when you came home?" Lauren asked.

"Nope. I had dessert first. And you know what? It was definitely worth the money. Chocolate mousse cake that melted in my mouth."

***

"Isn't it terrible?" A harried mother with a bursting to the brim shopping bag collapsed at the table Annie led her to. She spoke to her companion, who looked like an avid exerciser in her shorts and tank top.

"I know." The exerciser tutted. "And he was so young!"

"What are they talking about?" Lauren murmured to Zoe, as she slid the last batch of blueberry muffins into the glass case. She'd had to bake extra that morning because Ed wasn't working today.

"I don't know," Zoe frowned.

The café had only been open for fifteen minutes, but it was busier than usual. And those customers weren't the first to talk about something terrible happening.

"Do you know, Annie?" Lauren bent down to the silver tabby.

"Brrt." Annie sounded sad.

"Oh, she does know." Zoe clapped a hand to her mouth. "It's not Mrs. Finch, is it?"

"They said he," Lauren whispered.

"Oh – that's right. Phew." Zoe looked at her cousin in dismay. "You know what I mean."

"I do." Lauren's stomach sank. If only Annie could tell them who everyone was talking about!

"But how on earth did it happen?" A middle-aged couple walked past the counter, so engrossed in their conversation that they didn't notice that Annie hadn't greeted them at the *Please Wait to be Seated* sign. "Steve looked pretty healthy."

"Steve!" Lauren's eyes widened.

"Oh no!" Zoe looked shocked. "Not Steve. He was in here yesterday and seemed okay."

"He did look tired, though," Lauren said. "And I think he was worried about something."

"Maybe I should go to his house and check," Zoe suggested. "Maybe they're talking about another Steve. And he lives next to Mrs. Finch, so it will only take me a minute to run over there."

Before Lauren could say, "Good idea," the door to the coffee shop opened.

She turned her head, noticing that the background hum of shocked conversation had halted.

"Brrt?" Annie queried as she gazed at the entrance.

A tall man in his early thirties with short dark hair – cut a little too short, as if he didn't want to waste time with recurring trips to the barber – filled the doorway. He wore charcoal gray slacks and a white button-down shirt.

He was lean but muscular, as if he worked out regularly, and his presence seemed to command the room for a long moment.

Then the soft hum of conversation resumed, Lauren's customers returning to the business of perusing the menus at their tables, or taking a sip of their coffee or tea.

Lauren watched him stride to the counter. Her stomach fluttered – something it hadn't done in a while.

"Who is he?" Zoe whispered in her ear.

Lauren shook her head, mesmerized at his approach. He seemed so sure of himself.

"I'm looking for Annie." His voice was deep and masculine.

"Brrt?"

Lauren blinked, Annie's enquiry breaking the spell.

"I'm looking for Annie," he repeated, louder this time, his eyebrows drawing together in a frown. He had a straight nose and a mouth that didn't look as if it smiled enough. His serious dark brown eyes confirmed that impression. The whole package added up to one good looking guy, though.

Lauren cleared her throat. "This is Annie." She pointed to the Norwegian Forest Cat, then realized he probably couldn't see the tabby behind the counter. "Annie," she called softly, walking out from around the counter. Annie followed.

"That's a cat." His gaze narrowed.

"This is Annie," Zoe chimed in.

He raked his hand through his hair. "This is the Norwegian Forest Café, isn't it?"

"Yes." Lauren nodded.

"Then why would someone tell me to talk to Annie? Is there a person called Annie working here?"

"No," Lauren replied.

"And why is there a cat on the premises?" He frowned again. "Isn't that a health code violation?"

"This is a certified cat café," Zoe told him. "Although Annie *is* the only cat here. She seats the customers."

"Okay." He looked like he was humoring them.

"Who are you?" Lauren's curiosity won out over the butterflies in her stomach.

"Sorry." A tiny stain of crimson hit his cheekbones. "I'm Detective Mitch Denman. I'm investigating the death of Steve Quigan."

"So it *was* Steve." Zoe grabbed the edge of the counter.

"What do you know about the matter?" His gaze zeroed in on Zoe.

"We couldn't help overhearing our customers," Lauren said quickly. "They've been talking about an incident since we opened this morning."

"We heard the name *Steve* and I was just about to go over to his house to make sure he was all right, when you showed up." Zoe stood straighter and let go of the counter.

"What happened to him?" Lauren asked. "He seemed okay yesterday."

"He was here?" This time his gaze landed on her, making her cheeks heat.

"Yes," she replied. "He ordered a large latte to go."

He pulled out a small notebook and made a notation. "What time was that?"

"Around 10.30, I think."

"Did he order any food?"

"No." Lauren shook her head.

"What else can you tell me about him?"

"He drank a lot of coffee, and he was worried about something," Lauren said slowly, thinking back over her conversation with Steve, trying not to be distracted by the detective standing so close to her. "I think it was work related."

"I've been told he was an accountant," the detective said.

"That's right," Zoe replied. She scrutinized him, furrowing her brow. "Are you new to town? I don't remember seeing you before."

"Yeah, I'm new," he replied in a clipped tone.

"I think Steve was working on a job for the Episcopal church," Lauren said.

"Brrt!" Annie agreed.

"What did he do after you made his coffee?" he asked Lauren.

"He walked out of the café. I assumed he was heading home," she replied in a puzzled voice.

"Who found him?" Zoe asked.

"Pastor Mike." He checked his notebook. "He runs the Episcopal church."

"That's right," Lauren murmured.

"Apparently the vic—" he noticed their faces and rephrased "—Steve didn't turn up to an early meeting with the pastor that morning, and didn't answer the phone. So Pastor Mike drove over to the house, and saw him through the glass insert in the front door. He was lying in the hallway."

"Oh no." Lauren worried her lip.

"How did he die?" Zoe asked.

"We won't know for sure until the report comes back," he told them. "Did he say anything else to you while he was here yesterday?" His intent gaze honed in on Lauren. "Was he having a dispute with someone, or problems in his personal life?"

"He was divorced," Lauren said. "But as far as I know he wasn't having problems with anyone – apart from this work thing he was worried about."

"Thanks." He made a notation. "That's all I need for now, but I might be back later. When do you close?"

"At five."

Out of the corner of her eye, Lauren noticed Annie trotting to the entrance, where Hans, a dapper old man stood.

"Hello, Annie." His voice held a trace of a German accent. "Where should I sit today, hmm?"

Annie led the way to a small table near the counter, and hopped up on the chair next to his, as if reading the menu with him.

"Huh," the detective muttered. "Now I've seen everything."

CHAPTER 3

"I've been thinking," Zoe said later that day. They'd finally gotten a minute to chat, after being slammed with customers all day.

"What's that?" Lauren looked up from the blueberry muffin she was plating.

"Why did that detective ask us all those questions?"

"Because it was his job." Lauren had avoided thinking about *him* – Detective Denman – Mitch – all day – or at least had tried to.

"I think it was more than that." Zoe put a teapot on her tray. "If you ask me, it wasn't an accidental death."

"What are you saying?" Lauren frowned at her cousin. "Someone killed Steve?" She lowered her voice.

Zoe scanned the room but no one seemed to be looking in their direction. "That's exactly what I'm saying. What if it was … murder?"

Lauren instantly searched for Annie, relieved to see her snoozing in her cat bed.

"Are you serious?"

"As a dash of milk in a cup of tea," Zoe returned.

"Why would you think it was something sinister like that?" Lauren hadn't known what to think that morning when they'd been informed of Steve's death. Had it been an accident? Perhaps it was a heart attack, although Steve had looked pretty healthy – apart from all the coffee he drank. Could you die from caffeine overload?

"Because he – the detective – looked at us like we were suspects. At first, anyway."

"Isn't that his job?" Lauren had no idea why she was defending the man.

Her cousin had a point – she *had* felt like a potential suspect, especially with the detective's – Mitch's – gaze scrutinizing her, as if he were trying to see into the very depths of her. But she'd told herself she'd only been fanciful. It had been a long time since a guy had instantly caught her attention, and she was unaccustomed to the feeling.

"I guess," Zoe said grudgingly. "But I don't think he would have asked all those questions if it had been an accident. Plus, don't forget he didn't tell us how Steve died, did he? He said they had to wait for the report."

"You're right," Lauren said thoughtfully. "Maybe we should talk about this later, after we close."

"Definitely." Zoe slid the plate with the blueberry muffin on to her tray. "I'll take this over to table two."

"Thanks." The raspberry swirl lady from yesterday was at that table, but alone this time. Lauren hoped she enjoyed the muffin.

There had been no sign of Pamela, who had held court yesterday with her two guests. But that wasn't unusual. Some of her regulars only came once per week, while others, like Mrs. Finch, came in almost every day. That lady had popped in that morning, after the detective had left, and told Annie all about the commotion while she drank a cup of tea. Since Mrs. Finch lived next door to Steve, she'd seen and heard the police arrive.

Lauren hoped Annie would be okay – it might be too much for her if she had to listen to the customers talk about the tragedy. She glanced over at the shelf holding the cat bed – Annie slumbered, her ears twitching slightly. Perhaps a day at home tomorrow would be the best thing for the silver tabby.

"I'd better call my parents tonight," Zoe said as she returned to the counter. "I doubt it will make the news in San Diego, but I don't want them to worry."

"Good idea." Lauren felt guilty she hadn't thought of calling her Mom, who lived in Sacramento. If it was a slow news day, Steve's death could make the evening news and she knew her Mom would worry. She already fretted about Lauren running the café "single-handedly" and living in an old cottage, however well-maintained, despite Lauren reassuring her that Ed and Zoe worked at the café as well, and Zoe was her roommate.

She didn't think her mother had worried so much when Lauren lived fifteen minutes from her childhood home in Sacramento.

"And then we can discuss what happened today," Zoe said. "Over pizza."

"Okay." Pizza was one of Lauren's weaknesses, and the local pizza place made a near perfect one, *and* delivered. "But why would someone murder Steve?"

***

As Lauren opened the café on Tuesday morning, she thought back to her conversation with Zoe over pizza Friday night. Despite discussing the matter thoroughly, they hadn't arrived at any firm conclusions that it was murder.

They had finally decided to wait until they heard more from Detective Denman – Mitch, although Lauren half-hoped they wouldn't. That would mean Steve's death had been either natural or an accident – somehow – and it also meant that she wouldn't see the detective again.

On Saturday, Annie stayed home, only venturing into the café once, just as Mrs. Finch entered. After taking tea with her, Annie trotted down the hallway and through the cat flap to the cottage, seemingly glad to have an extra half-day off.

On Sunday, Lauren and Zoe hiked in the nearby Tahoe National Forest, a cool breeze ruffling their hair. On Monday, Lauren had done the grocery shopping and worked out a cupcake menu for the following week.

"Brrp?" Annie trotted over to the front door of the coffee shop.

Mrs. Finch tapped her way into the café, resting on her cane for a second.

"Oh, Annie." There was a note of distress in her voice. "I definitely need a cup of tea – and one of Lauren's cupcakes."

"Brrt." Annie brushed against the elderly lady's leg, then slowly led the way to a table near the counter.

"Are you okay, Mrs. Finch?" Lauren hurried over.

"Ed said the first batch of apple Danishes is ready." Zoe burst through the kitchen swing doors into the shop, then skidded to a stop. "You're early today, Mrs. Finch."

"You are open, aren't you?" The senior tried to smile.

"Of course," Lauren assured her. "What can we get you?"

"Oh, I've had the most dreadful morning," the elderly lady told them.

"What happened?" Zoe's eyes widened.

"Brrt?"

Lauren checked her practical white plastic watch – 9.35 am.

"The police knocked on my door this morning just before seven. They wanted to know everything about my relationship with Steve." Mrs. Finch's cheeks turned pink under her hastily applied orange rouge. "I told them I didn't have a "relationship" with him. He was my neighbor – and my friend."

"Good for you," Zoe murmured.

"But that didn't stop them. They said they had a search warrant to search my house – and garden. And just after Pastor Mike organized two nice boys to tidy up the wind damage from last week! The police tramped in, looked through things, and that detective who seemed nice last week asked me a lot of questions!"

"Brrt." Annie patted the senior's arm with her silver paw.

"Thank you, dear." Mrs. Finch smiled at the cat and stroked her.

"Then what happened?" Zoe leaned forward.

"Zoe!" Lauren admonished in a hushed whisper.

"It's all right, Lauren." A wobbly smile. "They combed through my garden and bagged up some bits of plants – not even asking permission! Then the detective said they were leaving, but they might come back at any time. And," she added indignantly, "not to leave town!"

"Wow," Zoe murmured.

"I told him, 'Where would I go, young man? I can't drive anymore, and I certainly couldn't walk to the edge of the city limits.'"

"What did he say?" Lauren couldn't resist asking. Surely there wasn't more than one detective in the small town? Mrs. Finch must be talking about Mitch.

"He said there are always buses and planes!"

"Oh dear." Lauren didn't know what else to say.

"Brrt!"

"Don't you worry about *him*." This time, Zoe patted her arm. "We'll make you a nice cup of tea and Lauren's baked a few different cupcakes today. And Ed's apple Danish has just come out of the oven."

"You do spoil me, my dears." Mrs. Finch slowly relaxed in the wooden chair.

"It's our pleasure." Lauren smiled, realizing she'd come to think of the elderly lady as a kind of substitute grandmother. How could Detective Denman – Mitch – even think the frail woman was capable of murder?

Mrs. Finch finally decided on a banana cupcake with chocolate frosting and a pot of Earl Grey tea. Annie stayed by her side as Lauren and Zoe hurried back to the counter.

"So it *was* murder," Zoe whispered as she spooned tea leaves into the pot.

"Looks like it," Lauren replied glumly. "Otherwise they wouldn't be going through Mrs. Finch's house and garden."

"Or asking her all those questions." Zoe shook her head. "Do you think we should suggest she hires a lawyer?"

"What?" Lauren stared at her cousin.

"It's what happens in all the crime dramas," Zoe explained. "If the police even *think* you *might* be guilty, it's best to lawyer up ASAP. That way you know what you should and shouldn't say. Even if you're innocent," she added hastily as Lauren continued to stare at her.

"I don't believe Mrs. Finch is guilty," Lauren stated. "Do you?"

"No," Zoe replied. "But what does the detective think?"

"Who cares what he thinks?" Lauren plated the cupcake with more force than necessary. *"I don't."*

"Okay, okay." Zoe held up her hands. "I just hope he doesn't arrest Mrs. Finch because he *thinks* she did it."

***

After Mrs. Finch had left, looking a little more cheerful, more customers trickled in until they were almost full by lunch. Usually, Lauren would be glad to see so many patrons on a Tuesday, but since the most popular topic of conversation was Steve's death, she wondered if it had been a good idea to open today.

Nonsense, she told herself. *If you were closed, then poor Mrs. Finch wouldn't have been able to spend some time with Annie, as well as fortify herself with cake and tea.*

She tried to forget about the police descending on Mrs. Finch's house – especially the detective in charge – and busied herself with attending to her customers.

Until …

"Oh no," Zoe whispered. She'd just finished making a cappuccino and was about to take it to the table when a tall, thin woman in her fifties walked in. Her hair was a dull brown and her outfit consisted of taupe slacks and a raisin colored sweater.

"Double oh no," Lauren murmured.

Ms. Tobin was one of the regulars – the only one Lauren wished *wasn't* a regular. She found fault with everything – apart from Annie.

"Brrt?" Annie trotted toward their most difficult customer, swiveled, and took her to a secluded table in the corner.

Lauren noticed the woman smile *very* briefly at the tabby, before sitting down.

"I'd better go over there," Lauren said. She knew from experience that Ms.

Tobin would not make her way to the counter to order.

"Okay." Zoe picked up the tray and carried the cappuccino to a table near the front.

All trace of good humor was gone from Ms. Tobin's face when Lauren reached the table. So was Annie.

"Is everything fresh today?" The middle-aged woman asked with a frown, tapping the menu.

"Yes, it is," Lauren forced her voice to sound cheerful. "I made all the cupcakes this morning, and Ed's apple Danish has just come out of the oven. And it's cool enough to eat," she added hastily.

"What sort of cupcakes?" Ms. Tobin peered toward the counter, but Lauren didn't know how she would be able to see the baked goods from such a distance. She knew *she* wouldn't be able to – unless she had binoculars.

"Banana with chocolate frosting, orange poppyseed, and vanilla."

The customer sighed. "Vanilla is so boring, isn't it?"

"Even with specks of real vanilla?" Lauren tried to keep her tone even.

"Maybe you should include that on the menu." Ms. Tobin pointed to the entry on the menu with a short, clean fingernail. "It just says, the cakes are at the counter. You should have a daily menu for the cakes and pastries. Then I wouldn't have to ask you what you're offering today."

Or you could walk over to the counter and look for yourself. Lauren didn't think there was any physical reason why this fifty-something woman couldn't easily walk the length of the café to view the sweet treats in the glass case.

But ... she didn't know anything at all about this customer, apart from the fact that she liked complaining. Maybe she had some kind of medical condition that limited her physically – yet during her days off, Lauren had seen her striding around the town. Perhaps she was just one of those prickly people who didn't like anyone. Even Annie didn't stay to "chat" with her – but did Ms. Tobin want the Norwegian Forest Cat to stay?

"No other pastries?" Ms. Tobin asked brusquely.

Lauren started, telling herself to focus. "Not yet."

She'd been so busy in the dining area that she hadn't popped into the kitchen to see what else Ed was baking that day. She knew he didn't like being disturbed – or being told what to make.

"What a shame." Ms. Tobin sighed again. "I suppose—" she paused "—I'll have an orange poppyseed cupcake. Give me the biggest one."

"They're all the same size," Lauren told her as politely as she could.

"And a large latte. Now, make sure you give me large. Not small, not regular. And I want two espresso shots in it. Don't give me a large that's full of milk and a single shot. It must have two shots of espresso."

"Of course." Lauren's pencil stabbed out the order on her notepad.

She hurried back to the counter to plate the order, knowing from experience that Ms. Tobin might time her. Sometimes she wondered if it was worth having that lady as a customer, but she didn't feel comfortable banning her. And what reason could she give? Because Ms. Tobin was a little rude?

Perhaps the middle-aged woman had an unhappy life, Lauren mused as she steamed the milk for the latte. Or perhaps she wasn't a very good cook, and that was why she came in at least once per week for a sweet treat and a hot beverage.

"All anyone is talking about is the detective and how good looking he is," Zoe grumbled as she joined Lauren at the counter. "Oh, and Ed said to tell you that he's making cherry pie and it's taking longer than he thought."

"Make sure you save me a piece," Lauren whispered, telling herself to ignore the first part of Zoe's conversation.

"Already did." Zoe cheered up. "And one for me, too."

Ed's cherry pie was legendary.

"How many is he making?" Lauren asked.

"Three. That's all the cherries he has. We should definitely charge more for his pie," Zoe suggested. "It sells out so fast."

"Would that be fair to everyone, though?" Lauren crinkled her brow. "I'd feel guilty if we charged Mrs. Finch more."

"We'd better save a piece for Mrs. Finch as well. I can take it to her house later. She needs extra cheering up after what happened this morning." Zoe's eyes narrowed as she studied her cousin. "I thought I might be imagining things, but I don't think I was."

"What?" Lauren placed the cupcake on the white china plate, careful that the tongs did not leave any sort on indentation on the unbleached paper case. Ms. Tobin noticed things like that.

"Whenever I mention the detective, your cheeks turn pink." She giggled.

"They do not!" Lauren felt as if she suddenly had sunburn.

"They do. But don't worry." Zoe put her hand to her mouth, as if she were trying to stop laughing. "I think he's noticed you, too."

"Really? I mean, why would you say that?" Lauren tried to backtrack.

"Caught you." Zoe unstifled her giggle. "It's okay. I don't like him in that way so we won't have a problem if you go for it."

"Go for what?" Lauren crinkled her brow.

"Go for what?" A deep, masculine voice asked.

Lauren's mouth parted as she looked up. *He* stood there –Detective Denman – Mitch.

Oh no!

How much had he overheard? She couldn't guess from his expression – it looked closed off and serious. He wore black trousers this time, with a cream button-down shirt. Lauren assumed it was part of his professional wardrobe, like capris, t-shirts, and sometimes an apron was for her.

Why hadn't she noticed him enter the café?

Where was Annie?

"Brrt!" Annie suddenly appeared, a scolding expression on her face, as if she were saying, "Why didn't you wait to be seated?"

Zoe snickered, then covered her hand with her mouth as the detective's gaze turned to her.

"I'll be in the kitchen." Her cousin fled.

Coward.

"Brrt," Annie repeated in an admonishing way.

"Why is your cat making that noise?" he asked. "Why isn't she meowing instead?"

"She's a Norwegian Forest Cat," Lauren informed him. "That's her way of meowing – or talking – although she can meow like a regular cat if she wants to. She can also purr."

"Huh." His eyebrows drew together as if assessing Annie. "She's an unusual cat."

"We like to think so." Lauren smiled at the silver tabby, positive Annie smiled back at her.

"Brrp!" Annie seemed to agree.

"What can you tell me about Mrs. Finch?" he asked abruptly, straight back to business.

Her mind flashed on Mrs. Finch's worried face that morning and she frowned.

"Why did you distress Mrs. Finch like that? Surely you don't believe that she—" Lauren swallowed "—killed Steve?"

"What do you know about it?"

"I know a frightened old lady came into the café this morning, after her house and garden had been ransacked." Lauren realized her voice had risen and she quickly looked around. But only a couple of patrons looked toward the counter.

"Does she come here often?" he asked.

"Practically every day," Lauren said, then wondered if she should have answered his question.

"Brrt?" Annie asked softly.

"It's okay." She bent down to stroke the tabby, glad to have a second to gather her thoughts. "Why don't you visit one of your favorites?" she whispered.

"Brrt!" Sounding happier, Annie trotted toward a table in the middle of the room, jumping on a vacant chair and causing a woman with glasses reading a book to show Annie the page she was up to.

"Is there somewhere private we can talk?" the detective asked.

Lauren glanced around. Most of the tables were occupied, a low buzz of conversation filling the room.

"I'll have to ask Zoe to cover for me."

He nodded. And waited.

Lauren's mind raced as she entered through the swinging doors into the kitchen. Zoe was doing the dishes, pink rubber gloves on her hands.

Ed was crimping the pastry edges on a pie. Right now, Lauren's nerves were too jangly for her mouth to water at the thought of Ed's cherry pie.

"Zoe," she hissed, not wanting to disturb her pastry chef.

Ed didn't look up, intent on perfection. Lauren knew from experience that once he was in the zone it was difficult to attract his attention.

"Has he gone?" Zoe looked up from the sink, a soap bubble on her cheek.

"No." Lauren wrinkled her nose. "He wants to talk somewhere quieter." She hesitated to say the word "private." "Can you cover the counter for me?"

"Sure." Zoe peeled off the rubber gloves and strode toward her. "Sorry I ran away like that, but there's just something about him that makes me wonder if I've committed a crime I'm not aware of and he's going to arrest me."

"I know what you mean," Lauren murmured, wishing she didn't. How could she be attracted to him? Maybe she should follow her cousin's example and explore online dating instead. Even if it hadn't worked out for Zoe – so far.

"Where are you taking him?" Zoe asked curiously.

"The hallway. If I don't reappear in ten minutes—"

"I'll save you." Zoe grinned. "Well, Annie and I will."

"Good." Lauren felt a little better.

Once Zoe stood behind the counter, Lauren gestured to the detective to follow her to the other side of the store. Parallel to the kitchen was a tiny hallway, and an unobtrusive door – with a cat flap.

"We can talk in here." Lauren unlocked the door.

Mitch followed her inside the narrow passageway. Lauren noticed he left the door open.

"Where does that lead?" He motioned to the yellow door at the other end of the small hall. It, too, had a cat flap.

"To my cottage," Lauren replied. "Annie can go home whenever she needs a break."

"That's clever."

"Thanks." Lauren caught herself smiling, and told herself to stop. "What did you want to talk about?"

"What do you know about Mrs. Finch?"

"She's a sweet old lady," Lauren answered. "I think she's lived here all her life."

"Have you?"

"No. I moved here a few months ago, when I inherited the café and the cottage."

"What about Zoe?"

"She moved here not long after I did," Lauren answered. "We're cousins."

"I didn't know that."

"But why are you asking about Mrs. Finch? I don't think she could hurt a spider."

"We've got the autopsy report back. The victim died of belladonna poisoning."

Lauren blinked, casting her mind back to college classes. "Isn't belladonna also called deadly nightshade?"

"Yes." He gave her a hooded glance. "Is there anything you'd like to tell me?"

"No."

A pause.

"Are you sure?"

"Of course I'm sure." Lauren straightened her shoulders. "Do you think I'm a suspect because I happen to know another name for belladonna? I'm sure a lot of people know that fact as well. Are they all suspects?"

"What else do you know about Mrs. Finch?" he asked.

"She lives alone." Should Lauren tell him the elderly lady could be a bit forgetful at times? Would that help or harm? "I haven't known her very long. She used to come to the café when my grandmother ran it."

"Your grandmother—" he raised an eyebrow, then noticed the expression on Lauren's face. "You inherited from her?"

"Yeah."

"Sorry." He sounded sincere.

"Thanks."

"The reason we searched Mrs. Finch's house is we need to discover who had access to belladonna. Her garden is overgrown at the rear, and we took a lot of samples. We're also checking the victim's neighbor on the other side of his house, if that makes you feel any better."

Lauren racked her brain. Who else lived next to Steve? Unfortunately, she came up blank. Obviously not someone who was a regular customer. Perhaps they worked fulltime, or commuted to Sacramento.

"Have you found anything?" she asked, not sure if she wanted to know the answer.

"Not yet," he replied. "Everything needs to be logged and sent to the lab. But, the victim – Steve – ingested the poisoning the night before he was discovered – or so the medical examiner says.

"And," he added, "it seems he drank some coffee with the belladonna."

"Coffee?" She furrowed her brow. "Why would you …"

"It could be suicide." He looked at his notebook. "You said he drank a lot of coffee."

"You seriously don't think he killed himself?" Lauren's eyes widened.

"We're not ruling anything out at this stage. And please keep what I told you just now to yourself." His lips tightened. "I shouldn't have told you as much as I have."

"But—"

"It's not as if it's an obvious murder, where he was hit on the head with a blunt object," he said brusquely. "He was poisoned. And now I have to find out if he killed himself, or if someone else did."

CHAPTER 4

After the detective left, Lauren barely noticed when Zoe told her in a disgruntled voice that Ms. Tobin hadn't left a tip – again.

Surely Steve wouldn't kill himself – would he? She didn't want to worry Zoe and Annie by voicing her thoughts, so she tried to concentrate on a new cupcake menu for the following week when she had a few minutes downtime between customers.

She didn't even enjoy Ed's cherry pie at supper as much as she usually did. Zoe had taken Mrs. Finch a slice, and had refused payment, saying she'd pay for it herself.

"Lauren?" Zoe waved a hand in front of her face. "Are you okay?"

"Just woolgathering – sorry." Lauren noticed Annie looking at her in concern as she sat at the table with them.

They were in Lauren's cottage, in the small dining alcove adjacent to the kitchen. Supper had consisted of the leftover paninis from the cafe, and the famous cherry pie.

"I'll cover the cost of Mrs. Finch's slice from the petty cash." She smiled at her cousin. "We might need to check on her a little more often with the investigation going on."

"Definitely." Zoe nodded. "Let's hope the police don't bother her again – and that they don't find anything incriminating."

"Brrt!" Annie agreed.

"I think we should talk about something else," Zoe declared after a moment. "Like my date tomorrow."

"Another one?" Lauren stared at her cousin.

"I know last week's date was disappointing," Zoe said, "but I decided to give it another try. We're meeting for burgers at Gary's Burger Diner tomorrow – that's okay, isn't it? I told him I could be there from twelve 'til one. That way if he's a dud, then I don't have to stay long. And I'll be back for the second half of the lunch-time rush which is the busiest time."

"Oh, Zoe." Lauren bit her lip at the thought of handling all the customers herself.

"I shouldn't have. Sorry." Zoe patted her arm, suddenly looking contrite. "I'll email him and cancel. I just thought Wednesday lunch at the café wouldn't be as busy as Thursday and Friday."

"You're right, it shouldn't be," Lauren told her. "But Ed's not working tomorrow so I'll be the only one on duty for a while."

"Oh, shoot, I forgot!" Zoe clapped a hand to her temple. "I'll definitely cancel and ask to reschedule. In fact, I'll do it right now." She whipped out her phone from her pocket and tapped away.

"All done." She showed Lauren the screen. An icon appeared.

"I think you've got a reply already."

"I have?" Zoe peered at the screen. "He says it's no problem and we can reschedule."

"What about tomorrow night?" Lauren suggested, feeling a little guilty at scuppering Zoe's plans, but feeling relieved she wouldn't be holding the lunchtime fort on her own.

A few seconds later …

"He said yes." Zoe sounded happy. "And his photo's not bad either. Want to see?"

"Okay." Lauren took the phone from her cousin. A guy who looked to be in his late twenties peered out from beneath a baseball cap. His features looked even and attractive.

"I hope his photo wasn't taken twenty years ago," Zoe muttered as she shoved the phone back in her pocket.

"At least you've got Rudy the rottweiler as an excuse now," Lauren reminded her.

"Maybe I should go on a date with Rudy," Zoe joked.

***

The next morning, Pastor Mike stood at the *Please Wait to be Seated* sign.

"Brrt." Annie scampered to the balding man's side. Lauren knew she liked the preacher.

"Hi Annie," he greeted the cat, a touch of sorrow on his face.

Whenever he visited the café, Lauren felt vaguely guilty that she didn't go to church more often.

"How's everything?" she asked as he approached the counter, Annie by his side.

"I can't believe Steve's dead." He shook his head.

"I know."

"He was auditing the church books," Pastor Mike continued. "He does it every year for us – free, even though I keep – kept – asking him to send us a bill, but he always said that was his way of giving something back to the church."

"Like a new coat of paint?" Zoe joined in the conversation. "Oops – sorry." Regret flitted across her countenance.

"You're right," the pastor admitted. "The church does need repainting. But it's a big job, and right now there doesn't seem to be enough money in the fund to cover it."

"Maybe you could have a working bee," Lauren suggested. "Everyone could pitch in. I could help on my day off."

"Me too," Zoe added. "It could be really fun."

"That's an idea," the pastor said thoughtfully. "I was waiting until Steve had gone through the books to work out what to do about money for the repainting but now …" he tailed off.

"Have the police released the work he'd done so far?" Lauren asked.

"No," Pastor Mike replied. "The accounting will just have to wait a bit longer. It waited last year too – Steve was due to go over the books a year ago, but got the flu, and somehow, we never got around to asking him to look at them until now. Pamela's been so busy with all her duties – I thought I'd take the burden off her and hire Steve myself this year."

"Pamela's the church secretary, isn't she?" Lauren queried.

"Yes, part-time," Pastor Mike replied. "We're lucky to have her." He sighed. "But now I'll need to speak to Steve's family and see if they'd like to hold the service here in Gold Leaf Valley."

"I thought he lived alone," Zoe said.

"He does. But he has an ex-wife in San Diego, and parents in Florida."

"Oh," Lauren and Zoe murmured.

After a few minutes of conversation, the pastor left with his regular cappuccino and a chocolate cupcake.

"I don't know if I'd like Pamela working for me," Zoe said, giving an affected shiver.

"I know what you mean," Lauren replied. "But she's probably very efficient in the church office and keeps everything organized."

"As long as she doesn't ever try to organize me," Zoe muttered.

Lauren knew Zoe disliked waiting on the older woman, but Lauren actually preferred waiting on Pamela to Ms. Tobin.

Hans entered the café, causing Annie to trot importantly toward the door to greet him.

"Can you help me find something, Annie?" He bent down toward the cat.

"Brrp?" she asked.

"My reading glasses – ach, I think I left them here."

Annie led him toward the counter.

"Did you say you were looking for your glasses?" Zoe asked him.

"Yes, I think I must have left them here on Friday."

"I didn't notice anything when I closed up last week," Lauren said. "Or since then."

"You haven't been trying to read without them all weekend?" Zoe asked. "You could have come over to the cottage to ask us if the café was closed."

"You are very kind." Hans smiled at them. "I only discovered this morning that they are missing when I went to the grocery store and needed them to read a label on a jar. You see, I have two pairs – one at home, and one in my coat pocket." He patted his brown wool jacket. "But my glasses are not in here today. And I stayed at home on the weekend."

"So you must have left them somewhere on Friday," Lauren surmised.

"Ja. And your café is the last place I visited." He bent down stiffly to the silver tabby. "Annie, we read the menu together, yes? I had my glasses on then. Do you know where they are now?"

"Brrt." Annie seemed to answer in the affirmative. She nudged Hans' hand, then scampered to her pink bed on the corner shelf. Jumping into her bed, she turned and nosed around the fleece-lined base, then patted something with her paw.

Lauren hurried over to the Norwegian Forest Cat.

"What have you got there?" Under Annie's paw was a black spectacle case.

Lauren picked it up. "Are these yours, Hans?" She returned to the counter, Annie by her side.

"Brrt!" the silver tabby said proudly.

"Yes, they are mine," Hans replied, opening the case and perching the glasses onto his nose. "Thank you, Annie."

"How did you carry them to your bed?" Lauren asked the cat. Surely her cat's jaws weren't big enough to carry the glass case.

"Brrp," Annie replied coyly.

"I don't think she's telling." Zoe laughed.

"Thank you, Liebchen." Hans stroked the cat.

"She must have spotted them and put them in a safe place," Lauren said.

"Annie's lost and found." Hans beamed at the tabby.

"Brrt!"

***

Wednesday's lunch rush was busier than usual, and Lauren was glad Zoe had rescheduled her date for that evening. After Annie had returned Hans' spectacles, they'd been slammed with customers.

A few patrons expressed disappointment that Ed hadn't created any pastry magic that day, although they seemed satisfied with Lauren's cupcakes, or her chocolate swirl coffeecake with streusel topping.

"Phew!" Zoe murmured once Lauren had locked up and turned the *Open* sign to *Closed* at five past five. "Today was amazing!"

"Do you think I should ask Ed if he'd like to work an extra day?" Lauren asked as she helped Zoe with the last of the dishes.

"Can you afford to?" her cousin asked.

"Yes." She'd been going over the sums in her head whenever she'd had a few seconds to herself that afternoon. "I don't want our customers to be dissatisfied."

"But the people I served said your cupcakes were awesome," Zoe encouraged her.

"Really?"

"Yes." Zoe grinned. "But if Ed wants to work on Wednesdays, that would be good, too. Less dishes for me."

"Oh, you." Lauren flicked a soap bubble at her. Although Ed's domain was pastry making, he also helped with general kitchen duties when he had spare time.

"Is there anything else to do?" Zoe turned serious as she drained the sink, a watery gurgle filling the air. "I'd like to get ready for my date soon."

"Of course." Lauren shooed her toward the cottage. "Go."

"Can you call me at 7.30 again?" Zoe asked. "Just in case he's not what I'm expecting."

"No problem. Do you want to take my car?"

Zoe started to shake her head, then hesitated. "Maybe I should."

CHAPTER 5

At 7.30 p.m. that evening, Lauren phoned Zoe.

"I wonder how her date is going," she said to Annie. They sat on the blue sofa in the living room, the TV muted.

"Brrp," the silver tabby replied.

Lauren wasn't sure if that meant Annie actually knew with feline intuition that things were okay, or if the cat was wondering as well.

Zoe picked up immediately.

"Are you all right?" Lauren asked. "How's it going?"

"What's that, Mom?" Zoe spoke. "Rudy's sulking and needs me to come home right away? Okay. I'll leave now." She hung up.

"What was that was about?" Lauren stared at Annie. "I hope she's okay."

"Brrt." Annie seemed to nod.

Lauren didn't have to wait long to find out. She heard her car stop outside, and then the slam of the front door. Zoe appeared in the doorway of the living room, spots of pink flaming her cheeks.

"Are you okay?" Lauren rose.

"I'm fine." Zoe flopped dramatically in the matching armchair opposite the couch. "Thank goodness you called me."

"Brrt?" Annie asked. She sat on the sofa, her ears pricked, waiting to hear more.

"He was eighteen!" Zoe placed her palm over her eyes.

Lauren's mouth parted but all she could manage was a feeble, "What?"

"I know," Zoe moaned. "That's it! No more online dating. I mean it this time."

"What happened? He didn't look eighteen in the photo you showed me."

"It was his brother's," Zoe replied miserably. "Apparently his brother doesn't know he stole it. And get this – he said he was going to ditch school to meet me on our lunch date. I don't want to contribute to the delinquency of am eighteen-year-old." She jumped up and paced the room. "But you and good old Rudy saved the day. He asked who Rudy was and I told him he was a huge rottweiler with slavering jaws who was upset because I hadn't taken him on the date. I left my share of the bill – we'd just received appetizers and I was counting the minutes until you called so I could leave with some kind of dignity. And," Zoe continued, "he said he was into older women!"

"Oh," Lauren murmured.

"I don't consider twenty-five to be old, do you?"

Before Lauren or Annie could answer, Zoe continued, "Although I suppose it is to an eighteen-year-old." She sank into the armchair again. "Why does this happen to me?"

"At least you're putting yourself out there," Lauren said. She admired that about her cousin.

"Not anymore." Zoe sat up straight. "I'm going to do something else – like – like—" her eyes lit up as she spied a magazine on the coffee table. On the cover was a photo of a woolen scarf. "Knitting!"

"Brrt!" Annie encouraged.

"I'm going to start a knitting club!" Zoe jumped up, excited.

"But you don't know how to knit," Lauren pointed out. "Neither do I."

"So, we'll learn." Zoe clapped her hands. "Ooh, I bet Mrs. Finch knows how to knit. She can teach us – no, she can be the guest lecturer! She wears woolen cardigans – I wonder if she made them herself?"

"I wonder," Lauren said thoughtfully. The cardigans did look homemade, but a good sort of homemade, not a raggedy effort like she suspected hers would be, even after lessons.

"And I'm going to knit … a blanket for Annie!"

"Brrt!" Annie sounded pleased.

"You'd like a pretty pink blanket to match your bed at the café, wouldn't you, sweetie?" Zoe asked the tabby.

"Brrt!"

"That's really nice of you," Lauren said.

"And a blanket should be easy – it's just a square or a rectangle. I bet I could whip it up in no time at all!"

"Maybe I could make a scarf." Lauren tapped the magazine in front of her – a woman wearing a red scarf with a fancy looking knitting stitch stared at her.

"Although maybe not as elaborate as this one."

"I'm sure Mrs. Finch can teach us the basics," Zoe said. "Ooh, we'll have to buy knitting needles and wool. I wonder if that handmade shop at the end of the road will have what we need?"

"You could check it out tomorrow on your lunchbreak," Lauren suggested. "And we can ask Mrs. Finch if she can teach us knitting. We were thinking of checking on her anyway, remember?"

"That's right." Zoe beamed. "I just know knitting is going to be so much better than internet dating!

***

The sound of metal pastry tins banging together filtered through from the kitchen to the café the next day. Lauren smiled. It was good to have Ed there, even if he only communicated to her with mostly grunts. She must find time to ask him if he'd like to work Wednesdays as well.

Lauren furrowed her brow as a sudden thought hit her. Mrs. Finch hadn't visited yesterday. She hoped the senior was okay. If there was a lull before lunch, she could hurry over to her house and check on her.

Before she could tell Annie her tentative plans, the door opened. She automatically smiled, ready to greet their first customer, when *he* walked in.

Oh no.

Her stomach dropped.

"Detective," she said politely.

"Ms. Crenshaw," Mitch returned, striding toward the counter, not even glancing at the *Please Wait to be Seated* sign.

"Brrt!" Annie scolded him.

"What can I – we—" she cast a glance at the silver tabby "—do for you?"

"I wanted to give you an update," he informed her.

"Oh?" she attempted to keep her tone noncommittal.

"After further analysis, we've come to the conclusion that the victim – Steve – was murdered."

"Oh no." She clutched the counter top. Lauren didn't know if that was better or worse than suicide.

"Brrt," Annie added sadly, her ears drooping.

"But how do you know?" Lauren asked.

"We went through his kitchen trash and found a coffee capsule that had been tampered with."

Lauren stared at him.

When she didn't say anything, he continued, "Someone had placed crushed belladonna leaf in the pod, added back the ground coffee, and glued on the plastic film that formed the lid."

"You're joking," she whispered, nervously looking at the espresso machine to her left. There wasn't belladonna in those beans, were there?

"I wish I were."

"But how did they – the killer – know for sure that Steve would use that capsule?" she asked.

"They didn't," he replied. "But there was a basket full of pods waiting to be used, right next to the coffee machine. The murderer couldn't be sure when the doctored pod would be used, but there was a good chance it would be – in time."

Who on earth could do such a monstrous thing?

"Why would someone kill Steve?" She cleared her throat.

"I don't know." He looked regretful. "Obviously someone who knew he drank coffee – and owned a coffee machine."

"That could be just about anyone," Lauren said. "Friends, neighbors, clients. He worked from home. Anyone who visited him and saw his kitchen would know that he had a coffee machine."

"Did you?" He scrutinized her.

She flushed. She didn't know whether it was from embarrassment at being considered a suspect, or because he was standing so close, with only the counter separating them.

"Brrt!" Annie said indignantly.

"Do you need me?" Zoe burst through the swinging kitchen door. "Lauren, are you – oh!" She froze when she saw the detective.

"Ms. Crenshaw." Detective Denman inclined his head.

"Do you need help?" Zoe whispered to Lauren.

"Did Steve own a coffee machine?" the detective asked Zoe.

"I don't know." Zoe wrinkled her nose. "I know he drank a lot of coffee, but I can't remember him mentioning he had his own machine."

"Hmm." The detective scratched in his notebook. After a pause, he said, "That's all for now, ladies."

Lauren numbly watched him leave. Annie muttered a grumble and headed toward the shelf. She hopped up in her bed and turned around three times before settling into a light snooze.

"I need to sit down." Lauren tottered to the nearest table and sank onto a wooden chair.

"What happened?" Zoe sat opposite her.

For once, the café was quiet. Although they'd just opened, the only sound she could hear was Ed banging in the kitchen. For once, Lauren was glad there weren't any early customers.

She told Zoe what the detective had shared with her about Steve's death.

"No way!" Zoe placed a hand over her heart. "I can't believe it!"

"I know." Lauren shook her head. "How could anyone even think up such a thing?"

"What else did the detective say?" Zoe leaned forward.

"That was all." Lauren shrugged. "You came in straight after that."

"I heard Annie and thought she might be calling for reinforcements. I guess she was."

They both turned to look at the Norwegian Forest Cat dozing in her bed.

"What about our coffee?" Zoe looked stricken as she turned to look at the espresso machine.

"That was my first thought. Mitch – the detective – didn't mention anything. But," she added, "I'm going to put those beans that are in the hopper in the trash – in fact, the remainder of the bag that's in the cupboard behind the counter. Luckily, we've got a new sealed bag in the storeroom in the locked cupboard."

"Thank goodness," Zoe murmured.

When she'd taken over the café, Lauren wondered if she'd been silly to lock up the extra bags of coffee beans, but now she was grateful she'd been so prudent. Not that Zoe or Ed would secretly help themselves, but she'd read an article online about a man pretending to work in a busy restaurant while stealing as much food as he could. She thought it best to be vigilant, in case a stranger wandered into the café kitchen.

"We'd better dump those beans now, while there's no one here." Lauren rose and headed to the espresso machine.

"And we'd better tell Ed not to let anyone into the kitchen – except us."

"Agreed." Lauren nodded. "We don't want to give the killer any opportunity to target us – or our customers."

***

At lunchtime, Zoe zipped off to check out the handmade store a block away, while Lauren held the fort. She'd eaten a hearty breakfast of bacon and eggs, so didn't mind having her lunch later, after the midday rush had lessened.

She could visit Mrs. Finch during her break. They'd been busy with customers ever since Mitch had left, but the elderly lady hadn't been one of them.

Forty minutes later, Zoe rushed into the café. "I've got it!" She brandished a brown paper bag. Gray metal knitting needles peeked out from the top. "I bought you some needles too, plus some wool. I got you red, like the color of the scarf on that magazine cover, and I bought a gorgeous shade of yarn for Annie's blanket. Look!" She pulled out a skein of ballet slipper pink.

"It looks great." Lauren smiled as she peered into the bag. She'd always thought Zoe had a good eye for color. The red looked just right – not too bold and bright, but not too dark verging on crimson, either. She just hoped she wasn't going to be all thumbs with the knitting needles.

"I'll go check on Mrs. Finch now," Lauren said, "if you'll be okay here."

"Sure." Zoe waved a hand in the air as she scanned the room. "Everyone seems to be occupied eating their lunch."

"Uh-huh." Lauren nodded. "And Pamela and Ms. Tobin aren't here."

"Even better." Zoe smiled mischievously.

"Annie's taking a break as well." Lauren glanced at the cat bed on the shelf where the Norwegian Forest Cat dozed. "She's had a busy morning seating everyone. Don't be surprised if she decides to go home for a while later."

"Okay." Zoe nodded. "And make sure you tell Mrs. Finch how we really want to learn to knit."

"I will," Lauren promised, glad to see her cousin enthusiastic about something that was safe and sedate. As long as she didn't wave knitting needles in the air and accidentally poke someone in the face!

***

A few minutes later, Lauren knocked on Mrs. Finch's front door. From this side, you couldn't tell that the police had tramped through her sweet cream painted Victorian house and garden.

Mrs. Finch had a small front yard with a neat lawn dotted with orange and yellow poppies. If the police had taken samples from those plants, they had done so unobtrusively.

"Who is it?" A quavery voice sounded behind the wooden door.

"It's Lauren, Mrs. Finch," she replied. "From the Norwegian Forest Café."

"I know who you are, dear."

The sound of a bolt reached Lauren's ears, and then the door slowly swung open.

"Zoe and I thought we'd better check on you. We missed you at the café yesterday – so did Annie."

"That's so thoughtful of you." She smiled. Dressed in a tan skirt and periwinkle blouse, her gray hair in a bun and leaning on her stick, she looked like the quintessential picture of a little old lady. "Do you have time to come in?"

"Thank you." Lauren entered the house. The hallway looked neat and clean with oatmeal colored carpet and lilac walls.

"I'm sorry I missed my visit with Annie yesterday, but the house was such a mess after the police trampled through it that I thought I should stay home and tidy everything up."

"Is there anything I can do to help?" Lauren asked. "I've got a few minutes before I'm due back at the café."

"That's kind of you, but I've just about finished." She ushered Lauren into the kitchen. It looked like a magazine picture from the 1960s, with pastel blue cabinets and countertops, and a darker blue linoleum floor.

"Wow," Lauren murmured as she took in the old-fashioned fixtures.

"I know." Mrs. Finch nodded. "Everyone says I should update, but really, why? *If it ain't broke don't fix it*, that's what my father used to say, and I think he's right. My husband and I moved here in the early sixties after we got married, and we were so happy." She smiled wistfully. "Leaving the kitchen the way it was is one way of keeping my memories alive."

"How long have you been on your own?" Lauren asked, hoping she was being tactful.

"Five years." The old lady sighed. "We were married for fifty-five years, and I have a married son who lives in New Mexico. He says he loves the climate there. But he calls me every week and visits on my birthday and Christmas."

"That's nice," Lauren murmured.

"You can see some of the back garden from here." Mrs. Finch pointed at a large window behind the sink. "They made a terrible mess." She tsked.

Small pieces of broken branches and some flower petals littered the lawn. Large trees grew against the fence, including an oak.

"Would you like a cup of tea or coffee?" She pointed to a black and chrome coffee machine on the counter top. "My son gave it to me for my birthday, but I don't know how to use it. He said all I have to do is read the instructions but I didn't like to hurt his feelings and tell him I don't drink coffee much."

Lauren's eyes widened as she took in the machine.

"Does it use pods?' she asked faintly. She walked toward it, needing to know the answer.

"Pods?" Mrs. Finch frowned. "I have no idea."

Lauren examined the appliance. "Yes, it looks like it does." She suddenly felt sick.

"Oh dear. You mean I have to buy pods in order to get coffee out of it?"

"Yes. You can buy them at the grocery store."

She scanned the kitchen countertops but didn't see evidence of any pods. If Mrs. Finch didn't know how to use the machine, or even know that she needed pods in order to use it to make an espresso, surely she couldn't have masterminded Steve's death?

"Do you need something to eat, Lauren?" Mrs. Finch asked. "You look a little pale."

"I'm okay," Lauren said hastily, racking her brain for another topic. She couldn't think about coffee and Mrs. Finch in the same breath.

"Zoe would like to start a knitting club and thought you might know how to knit."

"Yes, I do." She beamed. Then her smile faded. "But it's been a while." She held out her wrinkled hands, twisted with age. "I don't know if these old fingers can knit anything useful. Arthritis."

"Oh. But you'd still be able to teach us how to knit, wouldn't you? If you had time," she added.

"Yes, I think I would." Mrs. Finch sounded pleased at the idea. "And I've got plenty of time on my hands."

"Great. I'll tell Zoe. She's already bought needles and wool. When you come into the café next, you could discuss it with her."

Lauren refused to even think about the possibility of Mrs. Finch being a suspect in Steve's death.

"I'll be there tomorrow morning," Mrs. Finch promised.

Lauren said goodbye to the elderly lady, and hurried back to the café. Mrs. Finch couldn't be the killer – she couldn't even be a suspect, could she? However much Lauren wanted that to be true, she knew she had to tell Zoe about Mrs. Finch's coffee machine.

CHAPTER 6

"No way." Zoe stared at Lauren.

"I know." They'd just closed the café for the day, and Lauren couldn't wait any longer to tell Zoe about what she'd discovered at Mrs. Finch's house.

"I can't believe she would kill Steve." Zoe wrinkled her nose. "I mean, why would she? I thought she liked him."

"Me too," Lauren replied. "She mentioned to me once that he helped her change her lightbulbs when she didn't think it would be wise to climb the ladder to replace them herself."

"And Steve seemed a nice man," Zoe added.

"Annie liked him," Lauren said. "I did, too."

"So did I." A strand of Zoe's brunette hair swung forward, flopping over her eye.

"I – we – shouldn't jump to conclusions," Lauren stated. "Just because Mrs. Finch has a coffee machine—"

"And she doesn't know how to use it."

"—doesn't make her a suspect. If it did, then everyone in this town who owned an espresso machine would be considered suspicious."

"Yeah, because wouldn't the killer have to practice putting the belladonna in the pod and make sure that the glue they used was strong enough to hold the foil lid in place? Because the machine would have to extract the coffee and the poison without any problems or else Steve might have been alerted that something weird was going on."

Lauren shuddered.

There was a pause.

"We don't have a pod machine." Zoe brightened.

"And after what happened to Steve, I don't think I'll ever buy one." Lauren grimaced.

"I know what you mean." Zoe nodded. "I'm glad we're locking up the coffee beans when we close each night, and not leaving any out to use the next day."

"Yes." That was the new rule Lauren had implemented after learning how Steve died.

"I refuse to believe Mrs. Finch is guilty, though," Zoe declared. "I have to think that." She looked at Lauren. "Because I really want to learn how to knit. It's going to be my new thing."

"Not because you believe in her innocence?" Lauren asked wryly.

"That too," Zoe said hastily.

***

The next day, Friday, Lauren and Zoe opened up at nine-thirty. No customers poured through the door, so Lauren took the opportunity to show Annie a little pink mouse she'd bought for her after work yesterday.

"This is what Mrs. Finch gave you," she told the silver tabby, placing it on the wooden floorboard near her bed.

"Brrt!" Annie prodded it with a large paw. The mouse lay still. Annie hooked her paw underneath the fabric stuffed body and flipped it in the air. "Brrt!"

The cat pounced on the toy, then lay on her back with the mouse between her paws, moving her legs back and forth as if trying to disembowel the plaything.

"Hello," an elderly voice called out.

"Hi, Mrs. Finch." Lauren smiled and came to greet her, forgetting for a moment her suspicions of yesterday. "Annie is playing with a toy I bought her last night – I used your tip money from the other day."

"Oh, look at the darling." The senior beamed as she watched Annie play with the stuffed mouse.

"Brrt." Annie picked up the mouse in her mouth and jumped up to the bed. She placed the toy on the fleece lined base, then hopped down and trotted toward Mrs. Finch.

"Where should I sit today, dear?" Mrs. Finch asked the silver tabby.

"Brrt." Annie slowly led the way to the table closest to her bed. Lauren wondered if she was going to play with the toy with Mrs. Finch.

After taking her order of a pot of tea and a chocolate croissant, Lauren poked her head into the kitchen.

"Mrs. Finch is here," she told her cousin, who was washing up baking tins.

"Cool!" Zoe peeled off her rubber gloves and pushed open the swinging doors. She made a beeline toward the elderly lady's table.

Lauren watched them chat for a few minutes. Annie must have fetched her toy mouse, because she batted it across the table to Mrs. Finch while she and Zoe spoke. The elderly lady pushed the toy back to the cat, who immediately batted it forward again.

"Mrs. Finch said yes!" Zoe grinned as she joined Lauren at the counter. "She said we can come over after work today and she'll show us the basics."

"Good." Lauren smiled before remembering that Mrs. Finch might be a suspect. She lowered her voice. "You do still want to learn how to knit, don't you?"

"Of course." Zoe looked puzzled for a moment, then recognition dawned. "Oh, I see what you mean. No worries. I'll tell Ed what we're doing tonight, and then if we're reported missing next week, they'll know where to look!"

Lauren wished she could brush off thoughts of suspects and murder so easily.

You're being silly. Mrs. Finch is a sweet old lady who loves Annie. And Annie seems to love her. If she was a murderer, surely Annie could sense it in some way?

She looked across to Mrs. Finch's table. She was still batting the toy mouse to and fro with Annie. How could such a person be a killer?

The day passed quickly. After a slow start they were inundated with customers at lunchtime. At one stage, Lauren wondered if they'd even be able to close on time. But just as suddenly, their patrons left in the late afternoon, giving Lauren and Zoe plenty of time to close up by five.

"Phew!" Zoe wiped her brow dramatically. "I'm almost too tired to try knitting tonight – *almost.* I've been looking forward to it all day."

"Good," Lauren replied automatically. "I'll take Annie home and give her some dinner, then we can visit Mrs. Finch."

"We've got two caramel cupcakes left," Zoe said. "We could give those to Mrs. Finch – as a thank you for teaching us."

"Nice idea."

Zoe put the cupcakes in a cardboard box. "I can lock up and then I'll grab our knitting stuff. I think I left the bag in the living room."

"Okay." Lauren called Annie, and the silver tabby jumped down from her bed and ran toward her, the pink mouse in her mouth. "You like that toy, don't you?" she murmured.

A muffled, "Brrp."

Lauren fed Annie, and grabbed a glass of water.

"Found it!" Zoe entered the cottage kitchen brandishing the paper bag with the knitting accoutrements.

"Let's go." Lauren had been too busy that day to think any more about Mrs. Finch possibly being the killer. She decided to try and enjoy the knitting lesson – Zoe's enthusiasm would help.

They walked around the block to Mrs. Finch's house. Lauren carried the cupcake box while Zoe carried the bag of yarn and needles. The senior opened the door as soon as they knocked.

"Come in, come in." Mrs. Finch ushered them inside, her face alight with expectation. "I've been looking forward to this all day."

"That makes two of us." Zoe grinned.

Mrs. Finch directed them to the living room. The interior seemed more modern than her time warp of a kitchen, with beige carpeting and a fawn sofa with matching armchairs upholstered in a soft fabric.

"What would you like to knit?" she asked.

"I want to make a little blanket for Annie," Zoe took charge. "And Lauren wants to rustle up a scarf."

"Do you have the patterns?" the elderly lady asked.

Lauren and Zoe looked at each other.

"No," they chorused.

Lauren didn't think the magazine on her coffee table at home contained a pattern for the scarf on the cover.

"Never mind. I'll show you a basic stitch, called the knit stitch. This is the first stitch everyone learns. You can use this to make your blanket and scarf, or I can teach you stocking stitch, which some people call stockinette stitch, but that will involve learning the pearl stitch."

Zoe's expression fell.

"I'm sure Annie would love a blanket made just with the knit stitch," Mrs. Finch said hastily.

Zoe's face brightened.

Mrs. Finch showed them how to cast on several stitches, then encouraged them to try it for themselves. Lauren concentrated, feeling herself relax, even while her fingers fumbled with the strand of yarn she looped around the needles.

The tip of Zoe's tongue poked out as she followed Mrs. Finch's instructions – or tried to.

"Oh no," she muttered, as her knitting needles clashed together.

"Nearly there," Mrs. Finch said kindly, taking the metal needles from her and rectifying Zoe's error. "Try again."

Finally, Mrs. Finch deemed they both had enough stiches cast to start learning the knit stitch.

Another half hour later, they actually had a row of knitted wool on their needles.

"Now, just keep going along like that," Mrs. Finch advised them.

"I think I've got a hole already," Zoe groaned.

Lauren glanced over at her cousin's efforts. She thought there were two holes. Then she glanced down at her red knitted row. She *definitely* had a hole.

"Never mind, Zoe. Practice makes perfect," their teacher encouraged. "I'm sure Annie won't mind a few gaps. She'll be thrilled that you made a nice cozy blanket for her. Won't she, Lauren?"

"Yes," Lauren replied. She'd been so intent on mastering casting on and the knit stitch that her thoughts hadn't had time to stray to the subject of the elderly lady possibly being a murder suspect.

"If you're not happy having holes for your first attempt, you can always unravel and start again," Mrs. Finch continued.

"Start again?" Zoe looked horrified. Then she squared her shoulders. "I'm determined to learn knitting, Mrs. Finch."

"Wonderful!" The elderly lady smiled at her. "Why don't you come back next

Friday and show me how far you've gotten?"

"Deal. It will be our second knitting club meeting." Zoe blew a strand of hair that had fallen over her eye.

They left Mrs. Finch's house shortly after.

"I'm determined to get tons of knitting done tonight," Zoe said. "But I hope I don't get any more holes."

"Me too," Lauren replied.

"See? I knew Mrs. Finch couldn't be the killer," Zoe continued as they entered the cottage and greeted Annie, who was curled up on the living room sofa, cuddling the toy mouse. "How could a murderer be totally normal like that while teaching us the knit stitch?"

"I don't know," Lauren replied. Annie had plenty of toys strewn around the house, but right now seemed fascinated with only this one. Was there a reason for that? Or was it one of the innocent mysteries that came with having a cat?

"I'm starving." Zoe put down the paper bag containing their knitted efforts and headed toward the kitchen. "What should we have for dinner?"

***

Three hours later, Zoe flung down her knitting.

"Ugh," she moaned. "I don't think my fingers will work again."

Lauren glanced at her cousin's efforts. Three more rows, all of them with at least one hole.

"Why is yours better than mine?" Zoe snatched Lauren's handiwork and peered at it. Then she compared it to hers. "You've got less holes than me!"

"But your rows are longer," Lauren pointed out. "Maybe that has something to do with it." She wondered if she'd cast on enough stitches at Mrs. Finch's house. It might turn out to be a very skinny scarf.

"Maybe," Zoe considered. She yawned. "I don't think I can do any more tonight, though. But I'm going to knit some more tomorrow afternoon." She looked at her hands doubtfully. "If my fingers will let me."

"I'm sure they will," Lauren replied. "And I'm sure Annie will be happy with her blanket."

"Look, Annie." Zoe brightened and waved her knitting toward the silver tabby. "I'm making you a blanket!"

"Brrp?" Annie lifted her head. She sat on the armchair opposite the couch. Lauren thought it was a wise choice – no fear of enthusiastically brandished knitting needles coming anywhere near her.

The cat studied Zoe's efforts. "Brrp." Lauren thought it was an encouraging sound.

"Annie likes it." Zoe grinned. "Now I just have to finish it."

***

"I'm so sick of knitting." Zoe tossed her knitting down on the sofa. It was Saturday evening and they'd industriously worked on their knitting for the last four hours, the sounds of *click, clack, clash!* filling the living room.

"You've done a lot, though," Lauren remarked.

"But it's full of holes." Zoe scowled at her handiwork. "This blanket is going to have more gaps than actual stiches."

"You could always start again, like Mrs. Finch suggested," Lauren remarked. She'd thought of doing that herself. Would she actually wear this skinny scarf with its several holes and uneven garter stitch? It didn't look like the one the magazine model wore, that was for sure.

"Arggh!" Zoe hit her forehead with the palm of her hand. "Why did I want to learn knitting in the first place?"

"To keep your mind off guys – or the lack thereof of suitable ones."

"That's right!" Zoe jumped up, a determined look on her face. "And I'm going to do it, too – both things. No more online dating *and* become a knitting master." She blew out a breath. "I just need a break, that's all."

"I'm going to unravel mine." Lauren tugged the end of the wool and a whole line of garter stitch disappeared.

Zoe's eyes widened. "But what if you undo too much of it and lose your casting on stitches?"

"Then I'll try casting on again," Lauren replied calmly.

Zoe picked up her smushed blanket and scrutinized it. Then she let out a sigh.

"Yeah." She tugged out the metal needle and jerked on the pink yarn. "Goodbye, holes."

"Brrt?" Annie watched, fascinated, at the two piles of yarn. She hopped up on the sofa next to Lauren and patted at the dangling wool.

"Want to play?" Zoe held out a pink strand and suspended it in front of the cat. "Wheee!" She swung it in front of Annie.

"Brrt!" Annie jumped up and batted the yarn with her paw. She hopped over Lauren's lap and swung at Lauren's strand of wool. "Brrt!"

After a few minutes of playing, Annie yawned, hopped off the couch and curled up in the armchair, a sweet ball of silver-gray fur.

"Now I've got to start again." Zoe stared glumly at the knitting needle holding only the casting on stitches.

"At least you don't have to cast on," Lauren pointed out. She hadn't been so lucky.

"I'll do one more row," Zoe said. "And then we should talk about our plans for the weekend."

"What plans?" Lauren frowned. "We don't have any."

"Exactly."

Zoe's tongue poked out as she wound the wool around her finger, then clicked the needles together.

"I think we should do something fun." She paused between stitches.

"Like what?"

"Like going to a casino!"

"A casino? Really?" Lauren stared at her cousin.

"Yes! I've just read about a housewife the other day – I was waiting in line at the grocery store and picked up a magazine – and she won five thousand dollars at her local casino while on a girls' night out!"

"What did she win it on?" Lauren asked, interested despite herself.

"Slots."

"She was very lucky," Lauren remarked.

"Yep." Zoe nodded. "And we could be lucky, too!"

"Oh Zoe, I don't know. I don't have a lot of spare money at the moment."

"It won't cost much," Zoe said. "I'll pay for gas and we can visit the coffee shop or buffet there – a meal there shouldn't be expensive. And we could use some mad money to play with!"

"You've got mad money?"

"A little. I put a portion of my tips away into a fun money envelope. I'll use that."

"Hmm." Why hadn't Lauren thought of doing that for herself? She put her earnings away in a bills account and a savings account.

"We could go tomorrow," Zoe wheedled.

Lauren wrinkled her brow. "Tomorrow's Sunday."

"And the casino's open."

"Which one are you talking about?"

"There's a casino just outside Sacramento."

"How do you know?"

"I saw an ad when I was checking my email yesterday," Zoe said. "And I thought, that's got to mean something – first I read about that woman winning money at the casino and then I see an ad for a local casino."

Lauren glanced at her knitting – or what remained of it – a few stitches she'd managed to cast on.

"O-kay," she said slowly. "But not tomorrow. I already feel guilty about not going to church regularly – I'd feel extra guilty going to a casino instead of a church service."

"We can go to the casino on Monday," Zoe said quickly.

"And tomorrow we can go to church," Lauren said just as quickly.

There was a pause.

"Deal." Zoe grinned.

***

"You're right, the building does need painting," Lauren whispered to her cousin the next morning.

They'd put on some of their best church-going clothes for the ten o'clock service.

The wooden Victorian church had a steeple on one side, stained glass windows, and was covered in chipped, flaking ivory paint.

"I wonder who's going to audit the church accounts?" Zoe murmured as they walked along the paved path to the entrance. "Now that Steve's ..." her voice trailed off.

"I know." Lauren nodded.

They said hello to acquaintances who were already seated, then took a pew in the middle. Lauren glanced around, counting approximately thirty people.

Pastor Mike took the service, and preached about helping your neighbor.

"That's what we do," Zoe whispered to Lauren. "We help Mrs. Finch."

Lauren nodded, thinking Annie helped people, too. She'd noticed a lot of her customers' expressions light up when the Norwegian Forest Cat showed them to their table and spent some time with them at the café.

What did Lauren do to help her friends and neighbors? Maybe she could do more. But she wasn't quite sure where to start. She had two and a half days off per week, which was more than some people had, but she worked long hours as well.

She baked before the café opened every morning, and by the time she closed at five in the afternoon, she often didn't feel like doing much apart from playing with Annie, reading a book, or watching TV.

Maybe Zoe was right – maybe a fun day out was just what they both needed.

You could organize a working bee to repaint the church.

Yes! And if the church didn't have enough money to buy the paint, they could arrange a bake sale!

"And we're going to help Pastor Mike," Lauren whispered to Zoe.

When the collection plate came around, Lauren put in a decent amount, guiltily thinking of all the time she hadn't attended church lately. Zoe's eyebrow lifted as she saw her cousin's donation, then dug in her purse for a little more to add.

After the service, they said goodbye to Pastor Mike, who stood outside the church, shaking everyone's hand.

"I'd be happy to organize the repainting of the church," Lauren told him. "We could have a lot of volunteers to help us."

"Yes," Zoe smiled. "It could be a really fun day."

"That's very kind of you." Pastor Mike beamed at them. "Why don't I visit the café one day and we can talk about it then?"

"Great idea," Zoe said. "Hey! If you come in before we open, we won't be disturbed."

"Good thinking," Lauren remarked. "What about Tuesday, Pastor Mike? 8.30 a.m.?"

"I can make it." He nodded. "Thank you."

***

"We did our good deed yesterday," Zoe told Lauren as they drove to the casino the next morning. "We went to church and we're going to help repaint it."

"Pastor Mike is a good man," Lauren said as she drove along the highway. "He was very kind when Gramms died, and dropped by to check on me when I moved into her house afterward."

"I'm glad we're helping him." Zoe let out a whoosh of air. "And now we can enjoy ourselves today!"

About an hour later they arrived at the casino, a two-story brick building consisting of hotel rooms and a large gambling area.

After parking, Zoe grabbed Lauren's hand. "I can't wait to try everything!"

"How much mad money did you bring?" Lauren asked curiously.

"One hundred dollars. That should be enough, shouldn't it?"

"I hope so." Lauren had only brought fifty, and that included lunch money.

They walked along the redbrick path to the entrance. Ahead of them, a burly man came out of a side door and hurried toward the car park.

"Isn't that Ed?" Lauren stopped and stared.

"Where?" Zoe turned her head. "Yes, I think it is!"

"What's he doing here?" They looked at each other, their eyebrows raised.

"Maybe he read the same article I did," Zoe suggested, "and came to try his luck."

"But he looks – I don't know – not exactly happy?" Lauren frowned.

"Maybe he didn't win any money." Zoe waved in Ed's direction, but he didn't seem to notice.

They watched him open the driver's door of his ageing sedan and get in. The engine chugged, and Ed drove out of the parking lot, not appearing to see them.

"Huh. That was strange." Zoe shrugged and continued walking toward the casino entrance.

"Yes." Lauren wasn't sure what to make of it.

As soon as they entered the building, Lauren was distracted by the lights and sounds – and her cousin.

"Ooh – slots!" Zoe towed Lauren toward glowing machines featuring animated characters. Zoe plopped down on a red leather stool and pulled out five dollars. She fed the money into the machine and pressed a button. The reels whirred and came up – not a winner.

"Oh." Zoe pouted, then pressed the button again. *Ring, ring, ring!* She'd won two dollars.

"You should play too." Zoe gestured to the machine next to her, with red and white glowing lights. "Keep me company."

"Okay." Lauren sat down and opened her wallet. She'd decided on the drive here to stick to the minimums. She fed in a one-dollar bill and pressed the button to play the minimum of five cents.

Zoe was right. It was fun – at first. Her one dollar disappeared slowly, due to winning twenty or thirty cents here and there. Lauren glanced over at her cousin who was glued to the screen. Snatches of music and the simulated sound of coins pouring out of machines added to the entertaining ambiance.

"How much have you won?"

"I haven't." Zoe chewed her lip. "I've lost ten dollars."

"Oh." Lauren rose. "Maybe we should look around and decide what to do next." She glanced at her watch. "We've been here nearly an hour already. I know it's early for lunch, but I'm getting hungry."

"Me too." Zoe patted her stomach. "Okay." She peered at Lauren. "How much have you won – or lost?"

"A dollar."

"I need your self-control." Zoe sighed, then brightened. "But it's okay. I've given myself permission to use all my mad money today."

Lauren shook her head at her cousin's optimism, then followed her through the maze of slots to the other side of the room. Signs pointed to the bathroom, the buffet, coffee shop, poker room, and table games.

"Lunch buffet!" Zoe tapped Lauren's arm. "It's just opened."

"Let's go." Lauren's stomach growled.

They were the first patrons there. After paying, they wandered down the long line of food, the competing savory aromas teasing Lauren's senses. She found it hard to choose between fried chicken, baked salmon, sweet and sour pork, several Italian entrees, a few French dishes, an array of salads, and freshly baked bread.

Her eyes widened as they chose a table and sat down. Zoe's plate was piled high with a mish-mash of flavors.

"Are you going to eat all that?" Lauren stared at the chicken, pork, salmon, and beef bourguignon on her cousin's plate.

"Probably not," Zoe admitted sheepishly. "But I figured, why not try a bit of everything? I've already paid for it."

"Good point." Lauren knew if she ate so much at one meal, her pants would burst. She'd been thinking lately that maybe she should try to cut down sampling the sweet treats at the café – perhaps only having half a cupcake instead of the whole thing. So today, she'd chosen a small piece of salmon, two spoonfuls of sweet and sour pork, and green salad leaves.

"I'm glad you suggested this," Lauren admitted at the end of the meal, after dipping her spoon into a modest serving of passionfruit pannacotta, the velvety texture melting on her tongue. "It's good to have a change of scene sometimes."

"You know it." Zoe grinned. "And I think Annie is happy having a day to herself, too."

They'd left Annie in the living room that morning playing with her pink mouse.

"Definitely."

By now, there were a few more customers in the dining room.

"Check this out." Zoe picked up a flyer at the end of their table. "They've got bingo!"

"Isn't that for older people?" Lauren asked.

"So?" Zoe shrugged. "We can take a look and see if we like it." She waved the blue flyer in the air. "It doesn't say for seniors only."

"Okay." Maybe bingo would be fun.

They rose from the table, then Zoe gasped and quickly sat down.

"Quick, she'll see you!"

"Who?" Lauren looked around.

"Sit down!" Zoe hissed, panic on her face.

"Who is it?" Lauren stared at her cousin.

"Pamela!"

"Pamela our difficult customer?"

"Yes!"

"Where?"

"Over there," Zoe whispered. "But don't look!"

Lauren shielded her face with her hand and peeked through her fingers. Zoe was right. Pamela sat alone at a table, a plate piled with salad leaves in front of her.

"What's she doing here?" Lauren murmured.

"I don't know." Zoe scrunched her brow. "But I don't want to find out!"

"Why not?" Lauren asked curiously. "We're not doing anything wrong. It's not like we closed the café when it was supposed to be open to come and gamble."

"I know, but we were having a nice time and now *she's* here."

"It's not like she can ask us to make her a coffee or get her another plate of food," Lauren said.

"Can't she?"

Lauren studied the middle-aged woman again. Pamela looked up briefly from her salad and glanced around the room. Her gaze landed on Lauren.

Lauren smiled weakly and gave a little wave.

"Oh no," Zoe moaned.

"Come on." Lauren rose from the table. "We'd better be polite and say hello to her."

"I told you not to look," Zoe muttered as she trailed behind Lauren.

"Hi, Pamela," Lauren greeted their customer.

"Hello, girls," Pamela replied, not looking happy. She put down her fork. "What are you two doing here?"

"Having a day off," Zoe told her. "What are you doing here?"

Pamela looked surprised at the question.

"Having a day off as well, actually. I only work part-time for the church. I've heard that the lunch buffet here is good so I thought I'd try it."

Lauren glanced at Pamela's plate. It was full of healthy salad. Why would you drive an hour to try salad from a buffet?

"Have you won any money?" Zoe asked.

"What? No." Pamela seemed startled at the question. "Like I said, I only came here for the buffet, not to gamble." She peered at them. "How about you two?

Have you been playing poker or roulette?"

"No." Lauren shook her head. "We've only visited the slots area so far."

"But we're going to try bingo next," Zoe added.

"Well, have fun." Pamela nodded, as if dismissing them.

"Huh," Zoe grumbled as they headed toward the bingo room. "I can't believe she would drive all the way here just to eat salad for lunch. Who does that?"

"That's what I was thinking," Lauren said thoughtfully.

CHAPTER 7

When they readied the café the next morning just before eight-thirty, Zoe was still grumbling about not winning any money at the casino.

"At least you won fifty dollars at Bingo." Zoe cheered up at the thought.

"Yes, that was fun." Lauren smiled. She'd enjoyed Bingo more than she thought, wanting to play some more when Zoe grew bored and suggested they check out the table games.

Lauren had watched Zoe lose at roulette, and then suggested they go home. Her cousin had reluctantly agreed.

"And I still have twenty dollars of my mad money left, so that's something."

Lauren now had seventy dollars instead of her original fifty. She'd decided to follow Zoe's example and put it in a special fun money envelope for next time.

"It was weird seeing Ed there, though," Zoe continued, scrunching her nose.

"I know," Lauren said.

"What was he doing there?"

"Maybe he went there to gamble, like you said."

"Huh." Zoe pondered. "It was also strange seeing Pamela there."

"Maybe she was just having lunch like *she* said," Lauren said.

"Ooh, I know – maybe she was meeting a secret lover! The casino has hotel rooms."

"Zoe!" Lauren double-checked they were alone – apart from Annie walking from table to table, as if verifying everything was just right before they opened.

"What?" Zoe looked the picture of innocence.

"Pamela's divorced as far as I know. So why would she be meeting someone there?"

"Maybe *he's* married," Zoe suggested.

"We'd better not let anyone hear us talk about it," Lauren admonished. "Especially Pastor—"

"Hi, Lauren and Zoe." Pastor Mike walked in. They'd unlocked the door early for his arrival.

"Oops!" Zoe murmured.

"Brrt," Annie greeted him.

"Where would you like to seat us, Annie?" Lauren asked the feline. "We're going to talk to the pastor about repainting the church."

"Brrp," Annie replied in an approving tone. She led the way to a four-seater table near the counter, and hopped up on one of the chairs, looking at them expectantly.

"Would you like a coffee or a cup of tea?" Lauren asked. "On the house."

"And Lauren's made lemon poppyseed cupcakes today," Zoe said enthusiastically. "And since I haven't had any breakfast yet, I'm going to have one *right now*."

"That sounds delicious," the pastor replied. "But you must let me pay for mine."

"It's our treat," Lauren said. "You do a lot for the community. Let us do a little something for you."

Pastor Mike beamed. "That's very kind of you, Lauren."

Lauren and Zoe bustled behind the counter, quickly making lattes and plating cupcakes.

"I've been thinking," Lauren said, once they returned to the table. "If the church doesn't have enough money to buy the paint, we could hold a bake sale to raise funds."

"That's a great idea," Zoe said after hastily swallowing a mouthful of lemon poppyseed.

"It definitely is." Pastor Mike sipped his latte. "And I'll make sure I remember about that in the future if the church needs to raise money. I went through the accounts yesterday and there's enough for paint."

"Awesome!" Zoe grinned.

"Brrt!" Annie's ears pricked up and she looked like she was smiling.

"That's wonderful!" Lauren enthused.

"Are you still going to get the accounts audited?" Zoe asked curiously.

"I don't know," the pastor admitted. "Truthfully, I haven't been able to think that far ahead. Once the police release the work Steve had already done, I might be able to finish it myself. Otherwise, I'll have to find another accountant."

"So when should we hold the painting bee?" Lauren asked. "Zoe and I are off

Saturday afternoons, Sunday, and Monday."

"If we make it Monday, we can be there all day," Zoe added.

"I think it might take more than one day to get it all done," Pastor Mike said thoughtfully. "We'd have to get rid of the existing paint, then do two coats of paint. And some of the congregation work on Mondays, so they wouldn't be able to help."

He took another sip of his latte. "Why don't we make it a Saturday? You two could come once the café is closed, and that way I could possibly get a lot of the congregation who work during the week. If we can't get it all done on the day we could ask people to come and help again the following Saturday."

"Okay," Lauren replied.

"Brrt!" Annie agreed.

"We could make it this coming Saturday. And we could put a poster up in our window, so everyone will know about it." Zoe grinned.

"Brrt!"

"That would be wonderful," Pastor Mike said. "Thank you."

***

"Tonight I'll make the poster," Zoe said after the pastor had left.

"What about your knitting?" Lauren teased.

Zoe looked stricken for a second.

"Brrt," Annie added.

"I'll do some knitting after I make the poster," Zoe replied hastily.

"Let me know if you need any help making the notice," Lauren said.

"I thought I'd type it up on the computer and print it out. I'll use a huge font."

"Good idea." Lauren smiled.

"That's lucky the church has enough money to fund the repainting," Zoe mused as she cleared away their coffee cups.

"I know."

"Hey." Zoe paused mid-stride. "You don't think Pastor Mike is a suspect, do you?"

"What?" Lauren's eyes widened as she stared at her cousin.

"Brrp?"

"Maybe I shouldn't have said anything."

"Why would you think that?" Lauren frowned.

"Pastor Mike found the body," Zoe reminded her. "Steve was auditing the church accounts – what if there was something in there that the pastor didn't want him to find?"

"Like what?"

"I don't know." Zoe shrugged. "But what if Pastor Mike visited Steve that morning, knowing he would find his dead body?"

"No way." Lauren shook her head as she held the empty plates. "No way."

"Brrt." Annie seemed to agree.

"Why would Pastor Mike hire Steve in the first place if he had something to hide?" Lauren asked.

"Because that would clear him of suspicion," Zoe explained. "No one would think he killed the man he hired to audit the church accounts."

"I think you've been reading too many mysteries," Lauren countered.

"I did enjoy reading Nancy Drew as a kid," Zoe admitted.

"So did I," Lauren confessed. "But that doesn't mean I think Pastor Mike had anything to do with Steve's death.

"I'm just putting it out there," Zoe murmured. "I like Pastor Mike, too. But someone murdered Steve. And it wasn't us."

***

That night, Zoe whipped up some notices on Lauren's computer and printed them out.

"What do you think?" She showed her handiwork to Lauren and Annie.

Working bee at Gold Leaf Valley Episcopal Church Saturday April 21. Help Pastor Mike repaint the church and feel good doing good!

TIME: 9 AM.

Tell your friends!

"It looks great!" Lauren studied the big bold font.

"I'm going to put up three," Zoe said. "That's okay, isn't it?"

"Sure." Lauren smiled.

"Brrt!"

"Thanks, guys." Zoe grinned at both of them. She fetched her knitting from the sofa. "And now I'd better work on Annie's blanket. Don't forget, we're having the second meeting of knitting club on Friday."

"I guess I'd better do some, too." Lauren sat on the sofa and clicked her needles together with a sigh. "I don't think I'll ever finish this scarf." She'd only managed two rows with the new cast on stitches.

"Luckily it's not winter." Zoe giggled. "Because that's how long Annie might have to wait for this blanket."

"Brrt." Annie seemed to pout.

***

At Wednesday lunchtime, Pamela sailed in with a lady who looked familiar. Of course – Lauren mentally snapped her fingers – it was the raspberry swirl cupcake customer from last week.

Pamela wore a tailored twinset outfit and carried a snazzy black leather bag along with a smaller matching purse, while the raspberry swirl lady was dressed in a pastel floral skirt and cream top.

"Brrt," Annie said importantly as she trotted toward them.

"Thank you, Annie," raspberry swirl lady said as she followed Pamela and Annie toward a table in the middle of the room.

"Pamela's here," Zoe whispered to Lauren as she made a pot of tea for a customer.

"I know. I'll go," Lauren said. At least it wasn't Ms. Tobin. Now that she thought of it, she hadn't seen Ms. Tobin for a few days. She hoped the older lady was all right.

She headed toward Pamela's table, a smile pinned on her face.

"Why do you have posters in the window?" that lady greeted her. "It looks cluttered."

Lauren explained about Pastor Mike's repainting working bee that coming Saturday, wondering why Pamela didn't seem to know anything about it, unless Pastor Mike hadn't had a chance to inform her yet.

"What a good idea," raspberry swirl lady said. "Perhaps I could come and help."

"The more the merrier," Lauren encouraged. "I know Pastor Mike would appreciate it."

"What about you, Pamela?" raspberry swirl lady asked.

Pamela sighed with apparent regret. "I would love to," she said, "but I'm already committed to visiting my daughter that weekend. She relies on me so. Unfortunately, I'll have to miss the church service on Sunday as well. But if people had checked with me first—" she gave Lauren a pointed glance " —I could have suggested a more suitable weekend for the working bee."

"That's a shame," Lauren murmured.

"I suggested to the pastor that we hire professionals, but he's told me there isn't enough money to do that," Pamela continued. "It's such a pity."

Lauren escaped with their orders for chicken salad paninis, blueberry cupcakes, and a latte each, noting that Pamela had requested vanilla almond again.

It had been on the tip of her tongue to mention seeing Pamela at the casino two days ago, but perhaps she'd better not. It wasn't any of her or Zoe's business what Pamela did during her spare time. Although, apparently it did not include repainting the church.

"Did the two of them get together to gang up on us?" Zoe muttered out of the side of her mouth when Lauren returned to the counter.

"What?" Lauren scanned the room.

"Ms. Tobin at two o'clock."

Annie ambled up to the tall, skinny woman and led her toward a small table in the rear.

"I'll go." Lauren groaned.

"I owe you." Zoe flashed her a smile. "Seriously."

"You're making Annie a blanket, remember?"

"Uh-huh." Zoe nodded. "And I'll cook dinner tonight."

"Thanks," Lauren replied. She often didn't feel like cooking after a day baking and serving customers. "Can you make two lattes for me while I take Ms. Tobin's order? One's a vanilla almond."

"Sure. I'll just take this tray over to table eight and then I'll steam them up." Zoe winked.

Lauren headed toward the back of the shop. Annie had already departed from Ms. Tobin's table and was now greeting two new customers at the entrance.

"Hi, Ms. Tobin." Lauren said, her pencil and notepad at the ready.

"I'll have a large latte," Ms. Tobin said. Her face looked a little drawn.

"Are you okay?" Lauren asked. "We haven't seen you here the last few days."

"I haven't been well," the older lady admitted reluctantly. "A touch of stomach flu. But I'm okay now."

"That's good." Lauren smiled at her, realizing that Ms. Tobin hadn't instructed her on how to make the latte. Perhaps she still wasn't feeling one hundred percent.

"What do you recommend today?" Ms. Tobin asked.

"Cinnamon swirl cupcakes made with Ceylon cinnamon," Lauren replied. She was proud of the fact that she used real cinnamon, and not the more common Cassia cinnamon.

Lauren hurried back to the counter, picking up the lattes for Pamela's table from Zoe and dropping them off with the paninis and cupcakes, then busying herself making Ms. Tobin's coffee.

Zoe disappeared into the kitchen after she and Lauren scanned the room – no one was trying to attract their attention. Annie sat in her cat bed, washing her paw. Snatches of conversation reached Lauren's ears, but she was too intent on creating a perfect latte for Ms. Tobin to take any notice.

"Hey." A deep, masculine voice.

Lauren froze, then finished placing the latte on a tray. She looked up.

Detective Denman – Mitch.

"Hi." She cleared her throat.

"Are you busy?" he asked.

"Yes." Her gaze flickered to the tray in front of her with Ms. Tobin's order. "I'll just take this over to the table." She gestured toward the rear of the shop.

"Sure."

Lauren picked up the tray holding the cupcake and latte, hoping her hands didn't tremble. As if this day couldn't get any worse! First Pamela, then Ms. Tobin, and now *him*. She just hoped he wasn't here to interrogate her – again.

Lauren slowed her steps after delivering Ms. Tobin's order. She'd rushed around for part of the morning, making sure her customers didn't wait long. Since she doubted *he* would order anything, he could wait a few seconds. So why did she instantly feel guilty?

"Someone told me you serve the best coffee in town," he said to her when she returned. "I'll have a large latte—" he paused and eyed the baked goods in the glass case in front of him "—and a chocolate cupcake to go."

Lauren raised her eyebrows a little in surprise, but started making his coffee. Now would be the perfect time to ask him how the investigation was coming along – if she dared.

"How's the—"

"The repainting—"

They spoke at once. Lauren blushed. Mitch gestured for her to speak first.

"How's the investigation going?" she asked as she steamed the milk, a hissing sound from the machine punctuating her sentence.

"I can't talk about it right now," he replied.

"Oh?" She furrowed her brow. He'd been able to talk about it before – when he wanted information.

"It's ongoing."

"What about Mrs. Finch?"

"We're still investigating." His tone didn't give away anything.

"What about the church accounts?" she pressed, wondering at herself for her persistence. "Pastor Mike says they haven't been released yet."

"I was going to ask you about the repainting of the church." He dug out his wallet from his back pocket, and handed her some cash.

She rang up the sale, wondering what it was about him that caused those annoying butterflies to zoom around in her stomach.

"We're having a painting bee to help Pastor Mike," she told him, gesturing toward the posters in the window.

"Are you going?" he asked.

She slid the cardboard cup and a paper bag holding the cupcake across to him, careful her fingers didn't touch his.

"Yes, once we close here at lunchtime on Saturday. Zoe's coming, too."

"So the church has enough money for repainting?" he asked.

"Just enough, apparently," she replied.

Why was he asking her about it? Did that mean there was something shady going on with the church accounts, like Zoe suggested? Or was he just curious? Or nosy?

"Where's your cat?" he asked, looking around the shop. "She didn't greet me." People ate, drank, and talked to each other at the tables. A hum of conversation acted as background music.

"She's taking a break." Lauren gestured to Annie's bed. The Norwegian Forest Cat was curled up in a ball, her eyes closed. "Maybe she didn't think you'd like her saying hello to you. She's very attuned to things like that."

"I don't dislike cats. I've just never had much to do with them."

"Maybe you should tell Annie that," Lauren replied. "One day."

After Mitch left, Lauren realized he hadn't given her an answer about the church accounts. Had that been intentional? Or had he been caught up in their conversation as much as she had?

***

"Brrt!" Annie's break must have been over, because the silver tabby trotted up to Lauren after the lunch rush, looking concerned. "Brrt!"

"What is it?" Lauren bent down to speak to her.

"Brrt!" Annie scampered over to a table in the middle where Pamela and her friend had been seated.

The cat tapped the corner of a black leather bag that had been left under the table.

"It's Pamela's," Lauren murmured, picking it up. She remembered the older lady carrying it when she'd entered the café earlier. "Thanks, Annie." She stroked the tabby.

"Brrp," Annie replied, nuzzling Lauren's hand.

"I'll put it behind the counter and return it to her later," Lauren said.

"Brrt!" Annie sounded as if she approved.

The café was now half-full. Most of her cupcakes had sold out, which was very satisfying. She might even be able to close a few minutes early today.

"Do you need me out here?" Zoe came through the swinging kitchen doors.

"No, we're good." Lauren glanced down at Annie.

"What's that?" Zoe pointed to Pamela's black leather bag.

Lauren told her cousin what had just happened.

"You're so clever, Annie." Zoe stroked the silver tabby.

"Brrt." Annie seemed to agree.

"I thought we could return it to Pamela after closing," Lauren said, "since we don't have her phone number."

"Good idea." Zoe looked at the bag thoughtfully. "I wonder what's in it?"

"We'll never know." Lauren tapped the black leather. "Because a: it's zipped up and b: that would be nosy."

"And c: Lauren says we're not allowed to." Zoe pouted.

"A-ruff!" Annie chirped, which Lauren assumed meant, *D: "That's right!"* The feline didn't make that sound often, but when she did, Lauren knew she was asserting something.

"I'll come with you," Zoe volunteered.

"Are you sure?" Lauren asked, knowing how her cousin felt about Pamela.

"Why not?" Zoe shrugged. "It will be good to go for a walk after working inside all day."

Lauren looked out the window. The sun shone but she knew from popping outside before that it was chilly.

"Okay." Lauren bent down to Annie. "Would you like to come with us to Pamela's house later? Or would you like to relax at home?"

Annie closed her eyes for a moment as if pondering the question.

"Brrp, brrp."

"I think that means she'd rather stay at home." Lauren smiled.

"Brrt!" Annie looked at them in approval.

"I don't blame you, Annie." Zoe giggled. "Visiting Pamela isn't top of my list for things to do after work, but it will be something a little different."

Annie strolled back to her cat bed, while Lauren tended to the customers and Zoe returned to the kitchen.

Once their last customer had departed, Lauren turned the *Open* sign to *Closed* and locked the door.

"Nearly five." Zoe flopped down at a table, kicked off her sneakers and wriggled her feet. "Ahhh. That's better. Why did I agree to walk with you to Pamela's house?"

"Because you wanted to get outside in the fresh air," Lauren told her. "But I can go on my own if you'd rather."

"No." Zoe shook her head and jumped up. "Let's go. And then I have a date with my knitting."

"So do I," Lauren replied.

After taking Annie home and feeding her, Lauren and Zoe set off. Pamela had special ordered a large selection of Ed's pastries a while ago for one of her committee meetings, and Lauren had delivered them to her house.

"At least she doesn't live far," Zoe said, shivering a little in the late afternoon air as they passed Mrs. Finch's street.

"It is convenient." They turned into the road next to Mrs. Finch's. The backyards here backed onto the rear gardens of Mrs. Finch's street.

"Hey!" Zoe stopped as they reached Pamela's house – a posh late Victorian painted dark green. A neatly kept garden with a regimented row of pink and yellow hollyhocks met their gaze. She narrowed her eyes. "Pamela lives behind Mrs. Finch!"

"Really?" Lauren stood on tiptoes to get a better look at the garden behind the house. "How can you tell?"

"See that tall oak tree at the back?" Zoe pointed. "Mrs. Finch has one just like it."

Lauren craned her head and squinted at the large branches sporting green leaves. "Doesn't that tree belong to the house to the left of Pamela's backyard?"

"I think you're right. So that must be Mrs. Finch's house, one to the left of Pamela's in the next street." Zoe opened the green wooden gate and strode up the path, then stopped halfway and jumped up. "Yeah."

"I didn't know she was such a close neighbor," Lauren remarked.

"Poor Mrs. Finch."

"I wonder if she knows Pamela lives behind her," Lauren mused.

"I'll ask her at knitting club."

They rang Pamela's doorbell. A classical musical chime rang throughout the house. After a few seconds Pamela opened the door, looking surprised to see them.

"What can I do for you girls?" she asked.

Lauren held up the black leather bag. "Annie noticed you left this behind."

"That's right!" Chagrin flitted across Pamela's face as she took the bag from Lauren. "I completely forgot I had it with me."

Something clattered onto the doorstep. Small, black and white, and circular. Lauren caught a glimpse of three letters *C A S* – before Pamela scooped up the item and shoved it in her bag.

"I knew this bag had a hole in the lining." Her mouth pursed in annoyance, then she opened the door wider. "Won't you come in for some refreshment? I've got coffee – or tea, if you prefer."

Before Lauren could refuse, Zoe jumped in. "Thanks, Pamela."

Lauren raised a surprised eyebrow at her cousin while they followed the older woman down the hall. Why would Zoe accept Pamela's invitation? She guessed her cousin would fill her in once they left.

Pamela ushered them into a gleaming, modern kitchen that looked straight out of a magazine. Black and white dominated the space – and there was a fancy island with a sink in the middle of the room.

"Wow!" Zoe took it all in.

It was totally different to Mrs. Finch's kitchen, Lauren had to admit, but while Pamela's kitchen was stunning, Lauren preferred the hominess of Mrs. Finch's.

"Isn't it sophisticated?" Pamela smiled with pride. "Sometimes I entertain and I needed a kitchen that would allow me to make whatever quantities I needed."

"Where do your guests eat?" Zoe asked curiously, ignoring Lauren's frown.

"There's a dining room next door." Pamela waved a manicured hand toward the right. "The setup is perfect."

"You could run a café in here." Lauren spied a huge refrigerator and freezer, a six-burner stove, a double oven, and large microwave.

Pamela laughed, a tinkly sound that grated just the tiniest bit at the end.

"But I'm afraid I don't have a cat. That was a genius idea of yours, Lauren, to have Annie help in the café. A lot of people have told me the reason they visit your coffee shop is because of Annie."

Not because of my cupcakes or Ed's pastries? What about our coffee? Lauren's shoulders slumped a little.

"And I bet they keep coming back because of Lauren's cakes and Ed's pastries," Zoe said in a cheery tone, as if reading her cousin's mind. "I'd love a cup of coffee, please, Pamela."

"Of course." Pamela turned away from them and picked up a coffee press from the counter.

"Do you have a coffee machine?" Zoe asked.

"I'm afraid not, dear," Pamela's voice was muffled as she turned on the tap. "I can't abide them. Real coffee to me is from a press or from an espresso machine like you have in the café."

Lauren looked around, realizing there wasn't a kitchen table they could sit at. Zoe must have reached the same conclusion, because she scrunched her nose at her cousin. Pamela still had her back turned to them so missed their silent interplay.

"I must thank Annie in person next time I'm there," Pamela continued, "for discovering I left my bag behind." She spooned ground coffee into the pot.

"I can't believe Steve is dead." Pamela sounded sad. "He was a very nice man." She shook her head. "I don't know what Pastor Mike is going to do about getting the church accounts audited." She paused. "Have you two heard anything about the investigation?"

"Why would we?" Lauren frowned.

"Well," Pamela tittered, "I have heard that a certain detective has visited your coffee shop more than once."

"Because Steve was a customer," Lauren said, hoping her face wasn't flaming.

"That's right," Zoe added. "The café might have been the last place he stopped at, before ..." her voice trailed off.

"Oh dear." Pamela sounded contrite. "Perhaps I shouldn't have brought it up."

She handed them each a fine bone china cup decorated with flowers and gold edging. "Almond milk and sugar?"

Lauren and Zoe looked at each other.

"Why not?" Lauren ventured. Although she served nut milk for customers who requested it, she'd only tried it once.

"Here we are." Pamela opened the refrigerator and quickly poured the milk into a little jug before offering it to them. "I do like observing the social niceties."

Lauren wondered what the older woman would think if she saw the type of mugs Lauren and Zoe drank out of at home – thick mugs with stars, witty sayings, or just plain colors. Somehow

Lauren thought Pamela might shudder in distaste.

After they drank their coffee, which Lauren enjoyed, with notes of woody spices, and almond from the nut milk, she and Zoe said their goodbyes. Pamela hadn't invited them to sit anywhere, so they'd stood the entire time, and now Lauren's feet were begging to go home and lie down on the couch.

"So much for the social niceties." Zoe trudged down the street. "Our house mightn't be as fancy as hers but at least we'd offer her a seat – wouldn't we?"

"I hope so," Lauren replied. "Why did you accept her offer of coffee? I didn't think you cared for Pamela."

"I was curious and wanted to see what her house looked like." A twinkle of mischief sparkled in Zoe's eyes. "And she sounded like she was offering coffee to be polite, not because she particularly wanted to invite us in. So I thought, hey, why not?"

Lauren shook her head wryly as they turned the corner.

After a moment, Zoe spoke. "Did you see what dropped out of her bag?"

"It looked like a casino chip," Lauren said slowly.

"Ha! I bet she was having fun at the casino the same day we were there," Zoe remarked. "Because why would you drive all that way just for salad?"

"We don't know that she went there to gamble," Lauren cautioned. "That chip might have been stuck in the lining of her bag for years. Anyway, she could have lent that bag to someone – like her daughter."

"Okay, Mom," Zoe said good naturedly. After a moment, she added, "Do you think Pamela murdered Steve?"

"What?" Lauren nearly tripped over her feet as she spun around to face her cousin. "She doesn't have a coffee machine. How could she know the poisoned pod would work if she didn't experiment?"

"She says she doesn't have a machine. But she lives near Steve."

"So does Mrs. Finch but I don't want to believe she's the killer. And Mrs. Finch has a coffee machine."

"So you told me," Zoe replied. "But how could a sweet old lady like Mrs.

Finch be the murderer? She's teaching us to knit!"

"If you think the killer is someone who lived near Steve, then we might be suspects as well."

"What?" Zoe widened her eyes.

"Think about it. We live a block away from Steve. He was a regular customer. It's amazing in one way that the detective hasn't been back to the coffee shop more often." Not that she *wanted* him to, Lauren told herself – very sternly.

"You're right! I just hope the police don't think like I do."

CHAPTER 8

On Thursday, Lauren was just about to unlock the front door when Ed entered the cafe space. This was such an unexpected occurrence that she just looked at him, her mouth parting slightly.

"Can anyone come to the painting bee at the church on Saturday?" His short auburn hair stuck up in tufts and flour smudges decorated his black apron.

"Of course," Lauren told him. "I haven't been attending church much lately, but Zoe and I will be going when we close lunchtime on Saturday."

"Good." He nodded, as if wanting to escape back to the kitchen. "I was thinking I could give them a hand."

"I'm sure Pastor Mike would appreciate it." Ed was the gruff silent type, and most of the time she didn't know what to say to him, apart from how amazing his pastries were. She didn't think he spoke much to Zoe either, but Zoe spent a little more time in the kitchen doing the dishes, and was more accustomed to working with him.

"Pastor Mike's been good to me," Ed told her, "even though I don't go to church. I'd like to help him."

"We'll see you there, then." Lauren smiled. "Oh." A thought struck her. "Are you interested in working an extra day per week – on Wednesdays?" She hadn't had a chance to raise the subject until now.

Ed took a moment to reply. "Yeah, okay. But the same hours as the other days. It would really help me out right now – the dentist says I need a couple of crowns." He grimaced. "I even went to the casino on Monday to ask if they needed a new pastry supplier, or help in the kitchen on my days off here, but they turned me down."

"Oh." So *that* was why she and Zoe had seen Ed at the casino!

"I like working here," he said gruffly. "But I didn't know whether you could afford to pay me for an extra day, so I didn't ask."

"I can definitely afford for you to work on Wednesdays as well," Lauren confirmed, thinking it was sweet of Ed to be concerned about the café's finances.

Ed nodded, and ducked back into the kitchen. With his help, as well as the other volunteers – she didn't know how many were assisting, but she hoped it was a lot – maybe they could complete painting the church in one day.

She hummed as she unlocked the door. Annie jumped down from her bed and ran to the *Please Wait to be Seated* sign, ready to greet their first customer.

***

"Hi, Mrs. Finch!" Zoe waved her battered paper bag that contained her knitting. "I can't believe it's knitting club already!"

Lauren suspected her cousin was sounding a little cheerier than she actually felt that Friday evening. Zoe hadn't gotten much knitting done, despite her efforts. Neither had Lauren. At least now her scarf didn't look like it would become a skinny tie, but she was only a quarter of the way through her project. At the rate she was knitting, her scarf mightn't be ready until the winter after *next.*

"Come in, my dears." Mrs. Finch appeared glad to see them. Her wrinkled face creased into a smile as she ushered them into her house. It was a complete change from the way Pamela had greeted them when they'd returned her black leather bag. Although, Lauren admitted, it had been unnecessary for Pamela to invite them in for coffee. She and Zoe hadn't expected that.

"How is Annie?"

"She missed you today," Lauren told her.

Mrs. Finch sighed. "I wasn't feeling very well this morning, and I knew you girls were coming tonight, so I thought I would skip the café today." She brightened. "Maybe you could bring her with you next Friday."

"She'd love that," Lauren replied. Mrs. Finch was one of Annie's favorite customers.

"And she can play with our wool," Zoe added. "Annie loves doing that at home."

Mrs. Finch chuckled. "I'm sure she does."

They sat down on the fawn sofa, while the senior sat opposite them in an armchair.

"Now, how far have you gotten?"

Zoe pouted. "Not very far at all." She held out her knitting to the elderly lady.

"This is good, Zoe," Mrs. Finch said, a little surprise in her tone. "I can't see any holes at all."

Zoe beamed. "I really tried not to get any – and I was constantly checking after each stitch so I could unravel them right away, wasn't I, Lauren?"

"That's right," Lauren replied with feeling. Zoe's constant question of: *"Can you see a hole? Can you see a hole?"* had almost driven her *woolly* in the evenings.

"How's your scarf coming along, Lauren?" Mrs. Finch handed Zoe's knitting back to her.

Lauren showed the senior the beginnings of her project.

"Very good." Mrs. Finch smiled at her. "You two will be experts in no time."

"Awesome!" Zoe picked up her needles and started another row.

Lauren did the same.

"Have you heard from the police again?" Lauren asked, telling herself she wasn't asking because of *him* – the detective – Mitch – but because she was genuinely interested and concerned about the way the police had suspected Mrs. Finch.

"No, thank goodness." Mrs. Finch shook her head. "I just hope that's all over with now." Her eyes misted. "Poor Steve – he was such a good neighbor to me."

"What about his house?" Zoe asked curiously. "Do you know who inherits?"

"All I know is that he has an ex-wife and parents in Florida. And that he owned it – or at least was paying a mortgage. I don't know who will inherit."

They knitted in silence for a couple of minutes, the click clack sound of the needles almost soothing now.

"Hey." Zoe lifted her head from her blanket-in-progress. "Does Pamela live behind you?"

"Why, yes she does," Mrs. Finch replied. She waved a hand behind her. "One house over, though. How did you know?"

Zoe explained how Annie had discovered Pamela had left her bag behind. "Her coffee was quite good," she concluded, "apart from the almond milk. But I prefer the lattes and mochas we make at the café."

"That reminds me," Mrs. Finch said. "I poked around with that coffee machine again that my son gave me, but I still can't work out how to use it." She sighed. "I suppose I should pack it up and donate it to the thrift store, but if my son found out, his feelings would be hurt."

"I understand." Lauren nodded.

"All you need are some pods," Zoe said enthusiastically. "I could even buy some from the grocery store and see if I can get the machine working for you."

Lauren gave her cousin a surprised *"What?"* expression, her eyebrows raised.

Zoe bit her lip. "That's if you'd like me to, Mrs. Finch," she amended.

"That would be wonderful, dear." She beamed. "I'm sure I could get the hang of it once someone shows me how to make it work."

Zoe chatted to the elderly lady about the different types of coffee pods you could buy, although her tone was a little subdued. An hour later, when Lauren stated her fingers were beginning to get tired, they rose and said goodbye.

"Are you two going to the painting bee tomorrow?" Mrs. Finch asked as she saw them to the door.

"Definitely," Zoe answered. "We'll be there in the afternoon."

"I wish I could help Pastor Mike." She stretched out her gnarled, twisted hands. "But I would just be in the way. Do let me know how it goes."

"We will," Lauren promised. "Hopefully we'll see you tomorrow or Tuesday at the café. I know Annie will be pleased to visit with you."

"I'll be there as soon as I'm up to it." Mrs. Finch waved goodbye to them, before slowly shutting her front door.

Once they'd turned the corner into their street, Lauren halted.

"Why did you offer to help Mrs. Finch with her coffee machine?" She stared at her cousin.

"I know." Zoe wrinkled her nose. "I'm sorry. At that moment I wasn't even thinking she could be the killer and I just wanted to help her out. Like she's helping us with our knitting."

"I get it." Lauren bumped Zoe's arm. "I feel the same way." She paused. "If the police haven't taken her machine away, then I guess it's okay if we do help her learn how to use it."

"Yeah!" Zoe's eyes lit up. "Otherwise there would be a big yellow tape with the words *DO NOT USE OR ELSE* on her coffee machine."

Lauren chuckled reluctantly. "I'll come over with you when you show Mrs. Finch how to work her machine."

"Great." Zoe grinned.

Lauren couldn't match her cousin's grin. All she could think of was, *there's safety in numbers*.

***

The next morning, all their customers spoke about the painting bee at the church. Lauren didn't think they'd had so many orders for take-out before. Annie seemed disappointed – every time she tried to seat a new customer, they told her they wanted to go to the counter for a to-go order.

At eleven, Lauren bent down to the cat. "Would you like to go home?"

Annie tilted her head to the side, as if considering the question.

"Brrp," she finally answered.

Lauren walked her to the door leading to their private hallway.

"I'll see you before Zoe and I go to the painting bee."

"Brrp." Annie nudged Lauren's hand, then swished through the cat flap.

"We're almost out of cupcakes." Zoe studied the glass case that held only four of the sweet treats – all vanilla.

"Maybe it's true what Ms. Tobin said about vanilla being boring." Lauren furrowed her brow.

"No way!" Zoe patted her cousin's shoulder. "I love your vanilla cupcakes, and so does Mrs. Finch. Ooh, by the way, I didn't notice her come in this morning."

"Neither did I," Lauren replied. "And there's no way we – or Annie – would have missed her."

"Maybe she's still not feeling one hundred percent," Zoe said thoughtfully.

"I hope she'll be okay," Lauren said. "Maybe we should check on her later."

"Good idea. We could go to the grocery store tomorrow and buy some pods for her machine and take them over."

"Okay," Lauren agreed. "Should we go to church first?"

"I guess so." Zoe's tone didn't sound quite as enthusiastic.

"Maybe we should close up now," Lauren suggested. Their last customer had departed a few minutes ago.

"You're right." Zoe grabbed the last cupcakes and put them in a cardboard box. "We can have lunch first and then join everyone at the church."

Lauren felt guilty as she locked the door and turned off the lights. She'd never closed so early on a Saturday – it wasn't even noon! She hoped the desertion of customers meant that everyone was at the painting bee.

Lauren and Zoe used the private hallway to enter the cottage.

"We're home, Annie," Zoe called out. "And we're going to have cupcakes for lunch!"

"Brrt!" Annie sounded approving as she ran to greet them.

"And salad," Lauren added. "Then we're going to help Pastor Mike repaint the church."

"Brrt," Annie replied, weaving between their legs as they headed toward the kitchen.

Lauren gave the cat her favorite tin of fish, while Zoe plated the cupcakes.

"There's a bag of salad in the refrigerator," Lauren told her cousin.

"Okay." Zoe divided the salad into thirds – one third for her and two-thirds for her cousin. "Since you're so keen on salad," she told Lauren as they sat down to eat.

Lauren munched on a forkful of greens, wishing they hadn't sold out of paninis that morning. Oh, well. Less carbs. That had to be good – right?

After Annie ate her lunch, she trotted off to the living room.

"Probably cuddling up with our wool – or her pink mouse," Zoe guessed as she bit into a cupcake.

As soon as they'd finished eating, they said goodbye to the Norwegian Forest Cat and locked up.

"I know people say you don't need to lock your door in Gold Leaf Valley," Lauren said as she dropped the key into her jeans pocket and zipped it up, "but—"

"I know." Zoe nodded. "Especially with a killer in town."

"Oh, I forgot to tell you." Lauren touched Zoe's arm. "Ed is going to work at the café on Wednesdays as well." She told Zoe the reason they'd seen Ed at the casino.

"An extra day of Ed's pastries is awesome!" Zoe grinned.

They'd changed into old clothes – Lauren wore faded jeans and a white t-shirt that frayed at the hem, which she'd tucked in, and Zoe wore ancient chinos and a long-sleeved shirt with a pattern of arrows she'd picked up at the thrift store for a dollar, saying she was sure it would come in handy one day. It looked like this was its day.

Lauren's eyes widened when they arrived at the church. The grounds buzzed with members of the congregation wielding paintbrushes and cans of paint.

"Oh, wow!" Zoe stood still.

"I'm glad there are so many people here," Lauren murmured.

"Our posters must have worked!"

"Or else everyone wants to help Pastor Mike."

"Look, there's Ed!" Zoe waved to their pastry chef, who nodded in reply. He wore old jeans dotted with cream paint splashes and a plaid red shirt.

"Oh, no." Lauren's heart raced.

"What?" Zoe looked to the left, in the same direction as Lauren. "Oh."

Detective Denman – Mitch – wore faded black jeans that fit like a glove and a long-sleeved denim shirt. He was speaking to Pastor Mike, who looked like he was dressed in his oldest clothes, like his congregation.

"He did mention the painting bee," she muttered.

"He did? When?" Zoe peered at her.

"Wednesday. At the café."

"Do you think he's here to interrogate people or to paint?" Zoe looked at Mitch, her eyes narrowed. "He's picking up a paint brush. He's dipping it into a can of paint—"

"So I think we can assume he's here to paint," Lauren muttered through dry lips.

"Unless he's here to paint and interrogate at the same time!"

Lauren and Zoe stared at each other.

"Lauren and Zoe." Pastor Mike approached them. "Thank you for coming."

"Our pleasure," Lauren replied, shoving all thoughts of Mitch to the back of her mind. "What would you like us to do?"

"We've got a lot of work done already." The pastor beamed, seemingly unaware that he had a smudge of cream paint on his cheek. "But Mitch could use a hand over there." He motioned to where the detective attacked the side of the church.

"You don't have another section of the building that needs painting?" Lauren asked hopefully.

"Nope." Pastor Mike shook his head. "We're good."

Lauren trudged toward Mitch, Zoe by her side. "Stand between us," she whispered to her cousin.

"What?" Zoe looked startled. "Oh, yeah. You two have got the hots for each other but you're both pretending not to. Okay."

"Hi, detective." Zoe said breezily as they reached him. "Pastor Mike told us to help you."

"Sure." He looked at both of them. Was it Lauren's imagination or did his gaze linger over her? "We can share this tin of paint. And I see the pastor's given you brushes."

Lauren nodded, not sure if she could get any words out – *which was so stupid.*

Lauren eye-gestured to Zoe to stand between her and the tall, good looking detective. She edged away to the right as far as she could go while still painting the side of the church. If she could get into the zone, she'd be able to tell herself that it was only her brush, the paint, and the church.

Until she needed to load her brush with more paint.

Drat.

"Found any new suspects?" Zoe asked him chattily as Lauren edged towards the paint can, a sharp acrid tang hitting her senses.

"I can't comment on the investigation," he replied, brushing the cream paint neatly along the church wall. "How about you two?"

"What?" Zoe scrunched her nose.

"What?" Lauren frowned, forgetting for a second she was trying to pretend he didn't exist.

"I hope you're not interfering in police business," he told them, loading his brush with more paint. He looked directly into Lauren's eyes.

"Of course not." Her stomach tightened.

"We've got plenty of business of our own," Zoe said indignantly. "Cat café business."

"Good." He applied his brush to the wall. The wet bristles swished against the clapboard. "Why don't you open on Mondays?"

"Because it's our slowest day," Lauren said. "And it's good for Annie to have a break."

"We closed early today because we were sold out." Zoe's voice was filled with satisfaction. She gazed around the church grounds. People ate what looked like paninis and cupcakes. "I think just about everyone in town stopped by the café first to fuel up."

"Not everyone." He stopped painting and turned to look at them, his gaze locking with Lauren's.

Her breathing stopped.

"So why didn't you, detective?" If Zoe noticed the byplay between her cousin and Mitch, she didn't give any indication.

"I thought I'd get here as soon as I could to help," he replied, his gaze now encompassing the two of them and becoming more businesslike. "If there's another homicide, I might be called out, even if it's my day off."

"This is the first murder we've had since I moved here," Lauren replied.

"Good to know." He nodded. "How long have you been going to church?"

Lauren frowned at the question. "On and off for the last few months. Why?"

"Just wondering." He shrugged. "This morning, Pastor Mike kept telling me how great your café is."

"That's because Ed makes the pastries," Lauren said loyally.

"They are good," Zoe said dreamily. "He works Tuesday, Thursday and Friday, and now Wednesdays as well, if you ever want to stop in for one, detective."

"Zoe!" Lauren hissed. Her cousin sounded a little like an infomercial.

"That chocolate cupcake I had was amazing," he said.

Lauren blushed.

"Lauren makes the cupcakes," Zoe informed him. "But you have to try the vanilla ones – they're super awesome!"

The detective's eyes lit up. "I love a good hit of vanilla."

"You do?" Lauren glanced at him in surprise.

"Lauren only uses the best bourbon vanilla beans and extract. Did you know she adds vanilla seeds to the cake batter as well?"

"Zoe!" Lauren's voice was barely an undertone.

"Now I have to try one," Mitch said, his eyes gleaming.

"We'll be open on Tuesday." Zoe grinned.

"I'll see what I can do."

Lauren didn't know where to look – but she knew looking into his dark brown eyes would be far too dangerous. She edged away from him again, leaving Zoe in the middle, and attempted to concentrate on painting her section of wall.

She didn't succeed.

Not at all.

She kept sneaking glances at the man despite her best intentions not to. Once, Zoe caught her gaze and winked, a mischievous smile on her face. Great.

Sixty torturous minutes later, they were interrupted by Ms. Tobin, her slender form encased in a tan pantsuit and not a speck of paint on her.

Lauren was glad for any interruption – it meant she could focus on something else besides the detective's presence.

"What are you girls doing over here?" the older lady asked them.

"This is where Pastor Mike told us to work," Zoe replied, putting down her paintbrush. "We didn't see you when we came in."

"That's because I was over there," Ms. Tobin gestured to the other side of the church where several people wielded paintbrushes. "I was one of the first to arrive."

"I'm sure Pastor Mike appreciates your support," Lauren said.

"Why, yes, he does." The older woman's expression softened for an instant. "He personally thanked me this morning."

Lauren racked her brains for something to say. Perhaps she shouldn't mention Ms. Tobin being unwell earlier that week. She cast Zoe a *help me out* look.

Zoe returned her cousin's glance with one of her own: *I've got nothing*.

"You're welcome to help us here," Mitch's voice broke the awkward silence. "As you can see, we've got a lot of church to cover." He motioned toward the expanse of wall that needed painting.

"Thank you, detective," Ms. Tobin replied, standing taller, "But I was just on my way home. Pastor Mike said I've gone beyond the call of duty today," she added with pride.

"See you at the café," Lauren called after her, hoping her voice sounded cheery.

"Phew!" Zoe pretended to wipe her brow once Ms. Tobin was out of earshot. "I never know what to say to her."

"Me neither," Lauren said ruefully. "But we can't afford to offend any of our customers."

"Do you know her well?" Mitch asked curiously, dipping his brush into the paint can.

"No." Lauren shook her head. "But she seems to like Annie."

"But I don't think Annie has ever sat at the table with her."

"Does your cat sit with all your customers?" he asked.

"Only the ones she likes." Zoe giggled.

"But she shows all the customers to their table," Lauren added loyally.

"She sounds unique." He stroked paint onto the wall.

"She is," Lauren replied.

They painted in silence for a while, apart from the sounds of the brushes swishing against the clapboard. Lauren eventually relaxed – mostly – in Mitch's presence. It came as a surprise when Zoe put down her paintbrush and pointed to the late afternoon sun sinking toward the horizon.

"You've done a great job." Pastor Mike suddenly appeared, beaming.

"Thanks!" Zoe replied.

"There's only a little more to do and then the whole church is finished." There was a paint smudge on the pastor's other cheek now. "I can't believe so many people came to help today."

"You should," Lauren told him.

"Everyone likes going to your church," Zoe commented, before guilt flashed across her face. "Lauren and I are coming tomorrow,"' she added brightly.

"Wonderful." The pastor's gaze took in the section of wall they'd painted. "The three of you have got a lot done – you've really worked hard."

"Mitch started before us," Lauren felt impelled to say.

"But I couldn't have done all this on my own," Mitch remarked.

"We're going to pack up now," Pastor Mike informed them. "I'll be able to finish off the painting when I've got some spare time next week."

"I can stay a little longer and get more done," Mitch offered.

"That would be truly appreciated," Pastor Mike informed him, a smile wreathing across his face.

"We can stay as well." Zoe nudged Lauren.

"Yes." Lauren nodded, not sure if she actually wanted to stay any longer. Not when her nerves thrummed whenever Mitch looked her way.

"I'll have to buy Annie a little toy to say thank you for letting you stay," Pastor Mike offered.

"I'm sure she'd love that," Lauren replied. "But it's not necessary. We're happy to help."

"Mrs. Finch bought her one recently and she plays with it all the time," Zoe put in.

"Not that she doesn't already have toys," Lauren added hastily when she felt Mitch's interested gaze on her. She didn't want him – or the pastor – to think she was a bad cat mom and didn't provide Annie with any playthings.

"But she loves receiving new ones." Zoe grinned.

Once Pastor Mike departed, they returned to work. Lauren could hear the pastor's voice in the background, thanking each individual for their effort. Soon, the church grounds emptied, until it was only the three of them, or so Lauren surmised.

Zoe finally put down her brush with a splatter. "I'm pooped – oops! I didn't get anyone, did I?" Cream paint drops littered the grass.

"No." Lauren shook her head.

"No," Mitch replied. "You two go home and I can finish up here."

"Are you sure?" Lauren asked. His short brown hair was a little mussed and several dabs of paint decorated his denim shirt, but Lauren thought that made him look even more attractive. He looked like he was capable of working for a few more hours.

"Sure." He nodded.

They said goodbye, Lauren aware of how disheveled she must look after at least four hours of painting.

The further they walked away from the church, the more relaxed she felt.

"I think he likes you," Zoe sing-songed.

"I don't want to hear." Lauren clapped her hands over her ears, as if she were in elementary school.

Zoe giggled, then sobered. "Do you think that was weird seeing Ms. Tobin there this afternoon?"

"Not really," Lauren replied.

"But I didn't see her at church last week. Did you?"

"No. But she told me a few days ago that she hadn't been feeling well – stomach flu. She might have had it last weekend."

"Huh." Zoe continued to walk alongside Lauren. "How did she keep her outfit so pristine? Everyone I saw had splodges of paint on them." She looked down at her shirt which was covered with paint splatters. "Like me."

"I have no idea," Lauren said ruefully, noticing a new patch of cream paint on her t-shirt.

"I wonder why she's so dour all the time?" Zoe drew in her breath. "You don't think she killed Steve, do you?" Her eyes widened. "What if her stomach flu was actually belladonna poisoning?"

"What?" Lauren halted.

"She could have tested the poison on herself first, to make sure it worked!"

"Wouldn't that have killed her instead of upsetting her stomach?" Lauren frowned.

"I don't know." Zoe shrugged. "I haven't researched the effects of belladonna, *because I'm not a murderer*."

"But why on earth would she kill Steve? Did they even know each other?"

"I haven't seen them together. But someone killed him and an arrest hasn't been made so far, has it?"

"No," Lauren confirmed. "If someone had been charged with Steve's murder, it would be all over the café in minutes."

CHAPTER 9

The next day, Lauren and Zoe attended the morning church service.

"I don't see him," Zoe muttered, craning her head to check out the congregation sitting in the pews.

"Who?" Lauren asked.

"The detective – Mitch," Zoe whispered.

"Why would he come to church?"

"Because he likes you, silly. And he knows you're going to be here."

"Don't say that," Lauren muttered, picking up a bible and focusing her gaze on a passage about a shepherd and his flock. She'd been trying not to think about Mitch since she'd returned home from the painting bee and she'd succeeded – mostly.

Now, Zoe's comment made her look around the church to see who'd attended, but to her disappointment, she realized her cousin was right.

Pastor Mike thanked everyone again during the service for helping at the painting bee yesterday, proudly telling them that the work was now finished.

Warmth flickered through her at the thought that Mitch had stayed to complete the painting.

After the service, Zoe tugged on Lauren's hand. "We can go to the grocery store down the street, and then visit Mrs. Finch."

"Okay."

They trooped into the grocery store, Zoe making a beeline for the coffee aisle.

"These." She held up a red box of coffee pods. "Or should I buy these?" She picked up a navy box. "But they might be too strong for her."

They finally decided on a box of pods that boasted they were mild with a rounded balance.

"I don't think Mrs. Finch has ever ordered a coffee at the café," Lauren mused as they left the store.

"I'm sure she'll like these." Zoe waved the box in the air. "Ooh, we might be able to try them ourselves at her house – for testing purposes only, of course."

Lauren chuckled as they walked a few blocks to Mrs. Finch's.

"When we get the coffee machine working, we can go home and have lunch." Zoe yawned. "After all that painting yesterday, and church this morning, I think I'll have a nice relaxing afternoon doing nothing."

"I feel the same way," Lauren admitted. "I don't know if I even want to get in a few rows of knitting."

"I'm determined to finish Annie's blanket," Zoe said. "But maybe I'll have a break from it today."

They knocked on Mrs. Finch's front door.

A couple of minutes later, the door opened.

"Oh my," the elderly lady greeted them. "I'm very fortunate today with visitors." Her pink lipstick was a little smudged but otherwise she looked well put together. Her gray hair was in a neat bun, and her outfit consisted of an olive colored skirt and oyster hued blouse.

"We wanted to check that you were okay," Lauren said. "We missed you at the café yesterday."

"And we brought you some coffee pods." Zoe held up the box. "So we can get your espresso machine working."

"You're very kind," the senior told them. "I'm afraid I slept in yesterday, and by the time I was ready to visit you girls, I thought you might be closing a little early to help Pastor Mike at the church."

"We did," Zoe said. "We were slammed with customers early – and then they all left at once!"

"How did the painting go?" Mrs. Finch asked. "Oh, please come in."

"Everyone pitched in and Pastor Mike announced this morning that it's all done," Lauren said, following her down the hallway, Zoe on her heels.

Mrs. Finch clapped her hands. "That's wonderful! Wait until I tell Pamela."

"Pamela?" Lauren and Zoe chorused.

"Yes. She came for a little visit. Although we're backyard neighbors, we don't see each other often – she's so busy working at the church and steering her various committees."

"But I thought she was out of town this weekend," Zoe muttered out of the side of her mouth to Lauren.

"Me, too," Lauren whispered.

"Hello, girls." Pamela looked surprised to see them as she rose from the sofa in the living room.

"Hi," Lauren said politely.

"Did you hear that we repainted the church yesterday?" Zoe's gaze zeroed in on Pamela. "A lot of people turned up to help Pastor Mike."

"That's wonderful," Pamela replied.

"I thought you were out of town this weekend," Zoe blurted.

"Oh, yes." Pamela gave a tinkly little laugh. "I was in Sacramento yesterday, visiting my daughter. And I was planning to return home tonight. But my daughter got a call from work at eight o'clock this morning – some crisis apparently – and everyone had to go in on their day off. There was no point me staying any longer, so I decided to come home."

"We didn't see you at church this morning," Zoe continued.

Lauren nudged her cousin in the ribs.

"I was too late for the service. And I didn't want to disturb Pastor Mike in the middle of his sermons – he gives such good ones, doesn't he? So I thought I'd visit Mrs. Finch instead, and practice what Pastor Mike preaches about helping your neighbor."

"Why don't you sit down, girls?" Mrs. Finch gestured to the sofa. "There's plenty of room for everyone here."

"Thank you." Lauren sat.

"We came to fix your coffee machine." Zoe flopped down next to Lauren and showed Mrs. Finch the box of pods she'd bought. "I bet I can get it working for you."

"Coffee machine?" Pamela's gaze sharpened. "I didn't realize you had one, Mrs. Finch."

The senior explained it had been a gift from her son.

"And now we're going to help Mrs. Finch get it working!" Zoe jumped up. "Lauren and I can get started in the kitchen so we're not interrupting you and Pamela."

"I'm sure Pamela won't mind you girls joining us," the senior replied.

"Of course not." Pamela gave that tinkly little laugh again. It grated on Lauren's nerves.

Lauren rose, too. "It's no problem, Mrs. Finch." She smiled at the old lady.

"Well, if you're sure," Mrs. Finch quavered.

"We'll make you a cup of coffee," Zoe told her. "Would you like one, Pamela?"

Pamela shuddered. "No, thank you. I only drink coffee made in a press, or from a real machine, like in your café – remember?"

Lauren and Zoe headed to the kitchen.

"I hope Mrs. Finch didn't think I was rude," Zoe fretted as she plugged in the espresso machine. "But I wasn't expecting Pamela to be here."

"I know exactly what you mean," Lauren replied. She'd been a little disappointed that they hadn't been Mrs. Finch's sole guests. But surely it was a good thing to have her neighbors visit?

Zoe filled the water compartment and pulled the lever to reveal a space where she could drop in the pod.

"I knew I could get this working." She grinned.

"We'd better do a water rinse first," Lauren cautioned. "It might be a bit dusty inside."

"Good idea." Zoe turned on the machine. A loud growling hum filled the room. "Wow! That's loud."

"Maybe we've made the right decision not buying one of these for the cottage," Lauren commented. "I don't think Annie would like the noise."

"Yeah. She's used to the machine at the café, but it's in a much bigger space, so the noise is dispersed more," Zoe agreed.

Zoe dropped the capsule in, then grabbed a white cup from the mug tree nearby. "I hope Mrs. Finch likes this."

They watched as a thin stream of espresso poured into the cup.

"I'd better go and ask if she takes cream with it," Lauren said.

Lauren and Zoe had been so busy fiddling with the machine that they hadn't heard Mrs. Finch and Pamela talking. Now, as she headed toward the living room, Lauren wondered if they were having a pleasant conversation.

"No, I haven't heard anything more from the detective," Mrs. Finch said as Lauren hovered in the doorway.

"That's a shame," Pamela said sympathetically. "I mean, they could at least tell you if you're still a person of interest – I believe that's the phrase they use on all these crime shows."

"Sorry to interrupt," Lauren said. "Would you like cream and sugar in your coffee, Mrs. Finch?"

"That would be lovely, dear," Mrs. Finch replied. "Pamela, would you care for something? I could make you a cup of tea."

"Thank you, but I should probably go now." Pamela rose. "It's been wonderful talking to you, and I promise I'll drop by again soon."

Lauren returned to the kitchen as Pamela departed. She gave Zoe an update, and then prepared Mrs. Finch's coffee.

"It doesn't look like much." Zoe stared doubtfully at the tiny brown concoction.

"That's because we steam milk for lattes and cappuccinos, which creates more volume," Lauren replied. "But I didn't see a foaming wand or anything we could use to do that here."

Zoe carried in the coffee, Lauren following. "Here it is, Mrs. Finch. I can show you how to pop in a pod and make yourself an espresso after you try this."

"Thank you, dear." Mrs. Finch took the cup from Zoe and lifted it to her lips. After a couple of sips, she closed her eyes. "That is quite nice, Zoe. It would be fun if I could make one just like this." Her eyes fluttered opened. "Not that I wouldn't still come to your café, of course. I love seeing Annie and you two girls."

"Awesome!" Zoe smiled in relief.

"Now, you two must make yourself a coffee."

"Thank you," Lauren replied.

"We'll be back in a sec!" Zoe zipped to the kitchen.

"She's right," Lauren murmured a couple of minutes later, after tasting her own cream enhanced coffee. "Not bad at all."

"Pamela's totally missed out." Zoe giggled as she returned to the living room with her own cup.

They chatted with Mrs. Finch for a few minutes, then Zoe showed Mrs. Finch how to work the espresso machine, Lauren confirming Zoe's instructions when required.

Mrs. Finch made herself an espresso, seemingly delighted with her own efforts.

"We should be going now," Lauren said when the senior looked tired.

"Yes." Zoe nodded. "I've got to rest up so I can do lots of knitting this week."

"I hope you come to the café on Tuesday," Lauren said, pressing the senior's hand. "I know Annie will be thrilled."

"I will," Mrs. Finch said with determination.

They waved goodbye to the elderly lady, and power-walked home.

"I can't believe I'm hurrying so I can get home and put my feet up." Zoe chuckled.

"I know," Lauren said ruefully. "I'm just glad we're closed on Mondays – can you imagine getting up at six tomorrow and making cake batter?"

"Ugh." Zoe wrinkled her nose. "No, I cannot!"

***

Lauren and Zoe spent a relaxing Sunday afternoon chilling on the sofa. On Monday, they grocery shopped in the morning, including buying ingredients for the café, and knitting in the afternoon.

On Tuesday morning, Lauren put out a hand to stop the annoying *beep beep* of her alarm at six a.m. and stumbled into the shower, hoping the hot water would wake her up properly. Getting up early was about the only thing she disliked about running her own business. But if she had a job in Sacramento and commuted, she might have to rise at almost the same time.

Zoe chattered throughout breakfast, giving Lauren a detailed update about her blanket. She'd also given Lauren an update yesterday, while they'd spent a couple of hours knitting in the living room.

"I wonder if I can have it finished for knitting club on Friday?" Zoe mused, as she crunched on a spoonful of granola. "Won't Mrs. Finch be surprised?"

"Yes, she would," Lauren confirmed, wondering if she'd be able to finish her scarf by then. Probably not, if she wanted it to be a decent length.

"What do you think, Annie?" Zoe turned to the Norwegian Forest Cat sitting at the table with them and looking interested in their conversation. She'd already finished her breakfast of chicken in gravy.

"Brrt," Annie replied, her green eyes bright.

"I think that means she can't wait for me to finish her blanket!"

Me neither.

"We'd better get going." Lauren checked her watch. "I've got batter to make and cupcakes to bake. Ed's on today, and you know how he likes having the kitchen to himself."

"Do I ever," Zoe agreed.

They trooped down the private hallway to the café door, which Lauren unlocked.

"I'll set up the tables while you get baking," Zoe suggested.

Lauren whipped up a huge batch of cupcake batter. She hadn't made a cupcake menu this week, deciding to wing it. Today she'd planned on making chocolate and vanilla. And she definitely wasn't making vanilla because a certain detective had said he liked vanilla – not at all.

She'd just put a double batch in the oven when Zoe called out to her.

Lauren hurried into the café. Annie was in her cat bed, washing behind her ear, seemingly not concerned by Zoe's yell.

"What is it?"

"Look!" Zoe held out a blank white envelope.

"Where did you get that?"

"It was pushed under the door." They both stared at the front entrance to the cafe.

"Have you opened it?" Lauren asked.

"Nope." Zoe shook her head. "It's not addressed to anyone."

"Maybe there's an advertising flier inside," Lauren suggested.

"It's sealed." Zoe turned over the envelope.

"Maybe it's from a customer, asking us to save one of Ed's pastries for them."

"Could be." Zoe's eyes sparkled as she tore open the envelope. "Uh-oh." Her face paled.

"What?" Lauren peered over her cousin's shoulder. Her stomach dropped as she looked at the crude drawing.

A stick figure of a girl lay on the ground. The figure had a pixie hairstyle similar to Zoe's, but the color was light brown, practically the same shade as Lauren's. The figure wore jeans, a t-shirt, and an apron, a similar outfit to the ones she and Zoe sported.

"Anyone here?" Ed stuck his head through the swinging kitchen doors, scanning the café space. "Sorry I'm late." His gaze narrowed. "What are you two doing?"

Zoe wordlessly held out the drawing to him.

Shock skimmed his expression as he took it from her.

"Someone doesn't like you," he said gruffly.

"You think?" Lauren didn't mean for her tone to sound snarky.

"You'd better call the cops." He handed the drawing to Lauren.

"Brrp?" Annie trotted over to them, looking curious. "Brrp?"

"I think someone is playing a trick on us, Annie." Lauren bent to reassure the cat. "It's nothing to worry about." But the tension in her shoulders said otherwise.

"I'll get started with the pastries." Ed headed toward the kitchen. "Unless you want to close today?"

"No." Lauren squared her shoulders. "I'm not letting this – this—" she waved the offensive paper in the air "—stop us from serving our customers."

***

"Who could have sent it?" Zoe tapped her chin. They'd called the police as Ed had suggested, and were now waiting for an officer to arrive while they continued to get the space ready for their first customers.

Meanwhile, Lauren had frosted her cupcakes and put them in the glass case. She could really do with one now, but surely she could wait until her break?

"I don't even know if it's supposed to be me or you," Zoe continued. "The hair color doesn't look like mine, but the style doesn't look like yours."

"But the figure is wearing an apron, and the kind of clothes we wear," Lauren replied. "And since we're the only females who work here, it's a safe bet that it's one of us."

"Or maybe it's a composite!" Zoe's eyes widened. "It's supposed to mean both of us!"

"So why didn't they draw both of us?"

"Because they're really bad at drawing?" Zoe offered.

"Who thinks we're a threat?" Lauren posed the question.

"There's Mrs. Finch, Pamela, Pastor Mike, Ms. Tobin …" Zoe's voice trailed off. "I still don't think it could be Mrs. Finch. I wish she was my grandmother." Lauren knew Zoe's remaining grandmother had died a few years ago.

"I know what you mean." Lauren smiled mistily as she thought of Gramms. She wouldn't have swapped her for the world, but she viewed Mrs. Finch as a sort of substitute grandmother.

"I don't want to believe it's Pastor Mike," Zoe said. "Everyone in town seems to like him. Look how many people turned out to the painting bee. But he did suddenly have enough money to repaint the church, which is a bit strange."

"I know." Lauren sighed.

"Ooh - it could totally be Ms. Tobin. Yeah!" Zoe nodded so hard Lauren thought her head would fall off. "There's something about that woman – and don't forget she claimed she had stomach flu, right around the time Steve was killed."

"Maybe she's lonely," Lauren suggested.

"No wonder, if she talks to everyone the way she talks to us." Zoe snorted.

"Maybe that's just her way." Lauren shrugged. She'd given up trying to work out Ms. Tobin's behavior in the café. She seemed to enjoy complaining, but ate and drank everything she ordered. "She seems to like Annie."

"Everyone likes Annie." Zoe cast a glance toward the bed on the shelf, where Annie watched them, curiosity in her green gaze. "I bet whoever killed Steve liked Annie."

Lauren checked the clock on the wall. Nine-thirty. She unlocked the front door, her fingers trembling. She told herself she would not be intimidated by the crude drawing.

"At least the police have stopped badgering Mrs. Finch." Lauren had already told her cousin the snippet of conversation she'd overheard on Sunday between the senior and Pamela.

"Ooh, maybe the detective – Mitch – sent it to us! To warn us off solving the case! But that's a bummer if he's into you, Lauren." Zoe pouted.

"Do you really think he would do something like that?" Lauren crinkled her brow as she stared at her cousin.

"He *is* new to town," Zoe told her. "What if Mitch—"

"Are you talking about me?"

They'd been so intent on their conversation that they'd failed to notice the detective enter the café.

"You didn't wait to be seated." Zoe glanced at Annie, sitting in her cat bed.

"Brrt!" Annie chirped in an admonishing tone.

"What's going on?" He zeroed in on the piece of paper on the counter. "The station said you called and had something to report."

"This." Lauren pointed to the drawing.

He donned a pair of disposable gloves and carefully picked up the sketch. "When did you receive this?"

"It was under the door this morning." Zoe pointed to the entrance door that he'd just walked through.

"And it's supposed to be one of you?" He studied the drawing, then Lauren, and Zoe, in turn, his dark brown eyes assessing.

"I guess," Lauren replied.

"We thought it might be a composite – to mean both of us," Zoe added.

"I'll bag it for evidence." He carefully placed it in a plastic bag. "We can check for fingerprints and saliva on the envelope."

Zoe scrunched up her nose but didn't say anything.

"Have you shown it to anyone?" he asked.

"Only Ed," Lauren replied.

"How many people have touched it?"

"Zoe and me, and Ed."

"What have you two been doing?" he asked, raising his eyebrow.

"Nothing!" Zoe replied indignantly.

"It's true." Lauren nodded. She'd been racking her brains ever since Zoe had found the drawing. What exactly *had* they done?

"We've been going to knitting club," Zoe said.

"Who else goes?"

"Only us." Zoe grinned. "I created it recently."

"We were at the painting bee on Saturday, as you know," Lauren added. "But we didn't speak to many people."

"And we visited Mrs. Finch on Sunday," Zoe said, a look in her eye as if daring the detective to criticize them for doing so. "She hadn't been to the café for a couple of days."

"We wanted to make sure she was all right," Lauren forced herself to meet his measuring gaze.

"And is she? All right, I mean."

"Yes."

"Mrs. Finch said she'd come in today," Zoe added.

"Pamela visited Mrs. Finch on Sunday as well," Lauren said.

"Anything else?" Mitch asked.

"Not that I can think of," Lauren replied.

"I'll take this back to the station." He picked up the bagged drawing. "And I'll let you know if we find out anything." He turned to go, then halted, gazing at the cupcakes arrayed in the glass display cases. "You've got vanilla."

"Yes," Lauren replied. Had he remembered their conversation at the painting bee?

"I'll take one."

Lauren grabbed a paper bag, hoping her hands weren't trembling. It was just nerves from receiving that crude sketch, she told herself. When Mitch handed over her payment, she made sure their fingers didn't touch. She placed the bag containing the cupcake on the counter, so her fingers wouldn't graze his.

"Thanks." He smiled.

Awareness flared through her.

"Okay. Now I know for sure he likes you." Zoe patted her shoulder after Mitch left the café. "Did you see how he held the cupcake bag? Like it contained the most precious thing in the world." She sighed. "Why can't I find a guy like that?"

CHAPTER 10

After Mitch left, customers began to trickle in. Lauren and Zoe agreed not to tell anyone about the drawing.

When Hans, the dapper senior, came in around eleven o'clock, Annie trotted to greet him.

"Brrt." She appeared to be smiling up at him.

"Hello, Annie." He bent slightly to talk to her. "Where should I sit today, hmm?"

"Brrp," she replied chattily, leading him to a two-seater table in the middle of the room. She hopped on the opposite chair to his, and looked at him enquiringly.

Lauren watched the two of them "talk," and approached with her order pad, just as Hans rose a little stiffly from the table.

"I can get your order today, Hans," she told him. She gestured around the space. "It's not too busy right now."

"That is kind of you, Lauren." Hans smiled. "Annie seems to think a cappuccino and one of your cupcakes will be just right for me."

"I've got chocolate or vanilla." She scratched down the order with her pencil.

"Vanilla, please," Hans replied. "They are quite delicious."

"Thanks!" Lauren smiled. Another person who liked vanilla. Maybe Zoe was right about her vanilla cupcakes, after all.

"After this, I shall go on my daily walk and burn off the calories." He patted his slight paunch.

"Where do you walk?" Lauren was curious. "Do you go all the way to the park?" The small park was at the other end of town.

"No." He chuckled. "I do not think I could walk that far. I stroll around the neighborhood – a few blocks, that is all. The doctor said it is good exercise, and when you are my age, you must pay attention to the doctor."

"Did you see anything strange the day Steve died?" Lauren's pulse quickened. Why hadn't she and Zoe thought of this before? Someone out for their daily walk might be a witness and not even know it!

Hans closed his eyes for a moment, as if in deep thought.

"I did see something, yes," he replied. "But I cannot remember if it was on that particular day, or before then."

"What did you see?" Lauren held her breath.

Annie leaned forward in her chair, her ears pricked.

"I saw Pamela, walking up the path to Steve's front door. I did not think anything of it at the time, because she is the church secretary. I think a lot of people know he is doing the accounts for the church, yes?"

"Yes," Lauren replied, her mind buzzing as if she'd just downed a triple espresso.

"When I heard the sad news about Steve, I did not even think about Pamela visiting his house. It had gone completely – how do you say – out of my mind."

"I understand." Lauren nodded.

"I hope this detective finds the killer."

"Brrt!" Annie agreed.

It was on the tip of Lauren's tongue to tell Hans about the rudimentary drawing they'd received, but she held back. She didn't want to distress him – he looked unhappy talking about Steve's death.

"I'll get your order." Lauren bustled to the counter. She'd have to tell Zoe about Hans' revelation as soon as she had a spare moment.

After Hans departed, promising to come in again tomorrow, Mrs. Finch arrived. Annie greeted her with a delighted "Brrp!" and showed her to a table in the corner.

Lauren watched the elderly lady and the Norwegian Forest Cat say hello to each other, then came over to take the senior's order.

"Hello, Lauren." Mrs. Finch smiled up at her. Small patches of orange rouge decorated her cheeks. "I've missed Annie so much! We were just catching up."

"I could see." Lauren grinned. "What would you like, Mrs. Finch?"

"I think I'll try one of your lattes, dear." The elderly lady looked across the table at Annie. "What do you think, Annie? Should I have a cupcake or one of Ed's pastries?"

"He's made blueberry Danish today," Lauren told her.

"Brrt!"

"I think that means I should have a Danish," Mrs. Finch said.

"I think so, too." Lauren smiled at Annie. The cat's green eyes sparkled as she looked across at one of her favorite customers.

Mrs. Finch couldn't possibly be guilty of killing Steve – could she?

Lauren barely had a moment to herself the rest of the day. She took a hurried lunch break, but didn't have a chance to tell Zoe that Hans had spied Pamela visiting Steve's house.

Only when the last customer departed at a quarter to five, did Lauren sink down on a chair and let out a sigh.

"Phew!"

"I know." Zoe finished wiping down a table and joined her. She wriggled her feet with relief. "Let's just sit here for a few minutes before we finish cleaning up for the day."

"Deal."

Lauren closed her eyes. After a slow start they'd been slammed with customers. It was good for business, but not for her feet.

Her eyes flew open.

"I've been meaning to tell you this all day. When Hans came in, he told me that he saw Pamela visiting Steve one day."

"When?" Zoe jerked upright and slapped her hands on the table.

"Brrt!?" Annie looked at them from her cat bed, as if wondering what all the commotion was.

"He can't remember if it was the day Steve died or earlier."

"It was earlier," Pamela drawled. She stood at the *Please Wait to be Seated* sign, but Annie remained in her cat bed, her eyes suddenly narrowing.

Lauren froze with horror as she gazed at Pamela.

"Eeek!" Zoe squeaked.

Lauren clutched the side of her apron, sliding her hand into the pocket.

"I actually stopped by for one of Ed's delicious pastries. I've had a craving all day and it wouldn't go away. All the way here, I'd hoped you hadn't sold out. But now …" Pamela sighed dramatically, her eyes glittering like shards of ice.

"Now?" Lauren prompted, her heart hammering.

"I'd hoped my stick figure drawing would scare you girls off the case, but it didn't, did it?"

"*You* did that?" Zoe squared her shoulders.

"Yes. I admit I'm not an expert at sketching, but I didn't think it was too bad."

"The detective has taken it for evidence," Lauren told the middle-aged woman. "I'm sure he'll find fingerprints or DNA from your saliva."

Pamela gave a tinkling, grating laugh.

"You girls are just too much. Do you think I would make such amateur mistakes? Everyone knows these days all you have to do is wear gloves and use those self-sealing envelopes. No licking, no DNA."

Lauren and Zoe shared a look: *Help!*

"Someone might have seen you slip it under the door," Lauren challenged her.

"I doubt it." Pamela shrugged. "I left it here at two o'clock in the morning. I was the only soul around. And I know you don't have cameras inside – or out."

Lauren vowed to install cameras tomorrow – if she and Zoe were still here.

"How did you do it?" Zoe's voice barely quivered.

"It was an ingenious plan." Pamela laughed as she walked towards their table and looked down at them. "Poor Steve – such a fool. He wanted me to admit I had a gambling problem and promise I'd pay the money back."

Lauren drew in a sharp breath. "You were embezzling money from the church!"

"Embezzling is such a harsh word." Pamela frowned. "I *borrowed* it. I fully intended to pay it back. At first I did. But then I lost more and more, and I couldn't afford to repay it all at once."

"So when we saw you at the casino, you were there to gamble!" Zoe's eyes rounded.

"That's right. But after I spoke to you I went straight home. I was lucky you'd only been in the slots area and hadn't seen me except at the buffet. I prefer blackjack and roulette myself. When that little ball lands on my number—" she shivered in remembered delight "— there's nothing quite like it."

"How did Steve find out?" Lauren asked, fascinated despite herself.

"He was sick last year, and hadn't done the auditing," Pamela replied. "That's when I started falling behind with repaying the money. I had a long streak of bad luck. I was just turning it around this year when Pastor Mike suddenly announced he was bringing in Steve to do an audit. I'd been putting it off all year – it's easy to redirect Pastor Mike to some other task he should concentrate on, like hosting bible study two days per week instead of one, or inviting the poor folks in town to his place for lunch once per week."

"And he guessed someone was stealing?" Lauren pressed.

"You should be more careful with your words, Lauren." Pamela glowered. "I'd *borrowed* it. But Steve could tell there was money missing, and really, the only two obvious suspects were myself or Pastor Mike. And why would the pastor, if he were the guilty party, hire an auditor in the first place?"

"Mitch said there were belladonna leaves in the coffee pod that killed Steve," Lauren said.

"That was inspired." Pamela smiled – a creamy, self-satisfied smile.

A cold chill prickled Lauren's spine.

"I thought that up all by myself. It was easy. I knew Mrs. Finch had belladonna in her garden, although I don't think she realizes it. So I jumped over the fence kitty-corner – thanks to my aerobics class – and stole a few leaves one night. I crushed them up, and put them in a pod." She giggled to herself.

Lauren's hairs rose on the back of her neck.

"Guess what? When I told you girls I didn't own a coffee machine, it wasn't exactly true. I had owned one – but I got rid of it before the murder." Pamela's eyes gleamed with pride. "I needed to know if my idea worked – and Steve was the one who gave it to me in the first place! He was always drinking coffee, and he'd invited me over to his house to talk about the "predicament" and what I could do to make things right with the church funds, when he offered to make me an espresso from his machine. When I saw that it used pods, well ...

"I knew what I had to do. I bought a machine for cash in San Francisco so the purchase wouldn't be traced, a box of pods at a different store, and learned how to use it. Then I experimented with opening the pods, adding spices to them, gluing the lid back on and seeing if the coffee would still be extracted. And then ..."

"You graduated to trying it with belladonna," Lauren uttered in a shocked tone.

"That's right. And once I saw it worked, I made a poisoned capsule for Steve. But first, I got rid of that machine. I wiped it to get rid of my fingerprints and then I dumped it in a creek bed two hours away from here – in a different jurisdiction."

"Then what?" Zoe asked.

"I visited Steve, told him what he wanted to hear about how sorry I was about borrowing the church funds, and promised I'd pay back the money. We were in the kitchen, but I needed to leave the capsule there, so I pretended I heard the doorbell. He checked to see if someone was at the front door, and I dropped the pod into his basket that holds all his capsules, right next to the espresso machine."

"But wouldn't it look out of place with his other pods?" Lauren asked.

"You underestimate me, Lauren." Pamela's voice tinkled with sinister laughter. "When I was at his house previously and he made me an espresso, I'd mentally noted which brand of pods he used. In fact, he even told me. He went on and on about it – it's amazing he ever stepped foot in your café – he certainly liked making coffee from his machine."

"And then you waited until he eventually used the belladonna capsule?" Lauren put a hand to her mouth.

"That's right. He only took a few days to use it." Pamela sounded smug.

"How do you know what belladonna looks like?" Zoe asked curiously.

"High school science – a long time ago."

"So that was why Mrs. Finch said she thought something looked different in her garden!" Lauren exclaimed.

"I didn't think she'd be so observant." Pamela shrugged. "I thought I'd landed quite lightly in her garden."

"It wasn't just wind damage – it was Pamela damage!" Zoe stared at Lauren.

"That was why I visited her on Sunday," Pamela continued. "To find out if she knew anything about the investigation and if her arrest was imminent. She was the perfect suspect."

"But how could you?" Lauren stared at the sleek, middle-aged woman. "Mrs. Finch hasn't harmed anyone."

"No," Pamela relied. "But I certainly didn't want to be arrested, did I?"

"Were you really at your daughter's last weekend?" Zoe asked. "Or were you lurking around town?"

"I *was* at my daughter's," Pamela replied. "Anything to get out of repainting the church." She shuddered. "I don't like manual work. I told Pastor Mike before to hire professionals to repaint it, but …"

"There wasn't enough money because you sto – borrowed it," Lauren murmured, not wanting to rile Pamela further.

"That's right." Pamela nodded. "Somehow he managed to get a big discount on the paint from the hardware store – a returned order – which was the only way he could afford to repaint the church, with everyone helping." She shuddered.

"I'd planned to stay the whole weekend with my daughter, so what I'd told you about being out of town wasn't a lie, but at breakfast on Sunday morning my daughter saw a small article about Steve's murder in a Sacramento newspaper – she never gets rid of them right away – and I became worried about the investigation, so I cut my visit short with her and dropped by Mrs. Finch's house."

"And?" Zoe asked.

"It looks like the police aren't going to arrest her," Pamela replied in a disgusted tone. "And then I heard from Ms. Tobin yesterday that you were at the painting bee, speaking to the detective – for a long time."

"Pastor Mike told us to help him," Lauren replied, drawing herself up straight.

"We barely talked about the murder," Zoe added indignantly.

"I couldn't risk it." Pamela shook her head. "Not after you saw me at the casino – and then that casino chip dropped out of my bag when you returned it to me. That's why I sent you the drawing to scare you off."

"You didn't," Lauren said stoutly.

"Yeah!"

"Purrr. Purrr. Purrr." Until now Annie had been silent, but now she stood in her bed, arching her back, her fur spiking. Her purrs sounded ferocious. She looked ready to spring into action!

"Annie doesn't scare me." Pamela tossed off a laugh but Lauren noted it didn't ring true.

"She knows you're not here in a friendly way," Lauren told her. "I'm going to call the police right now." She dug her phone out of her apron pocket and hit 911. "We're witnesses to your confession."

"Oh, no, you don't!" Pamela lunged for the phone.

Lauren screamed and scooted backward on the chair. She and the chair tipped over on the floor, the phone skittering across the floor toward Annie. The Norwegian Forest Cat flew down from the bed, picked up the small device, and jumped back onto her bed. She placed her paws over the phone, as if she were guarding it with her life.

Lauren picked up the wooden chair and held it between herself and Pamela, as if fending off a tiger.

"Get the phone from Annie," she gasped to Zoe.

Zoe half-crouched, half-ran to the cat bed and grabbed the phone.

"Hurry, please," she gasped as her 911 call connected. "The Norwegian Forest Café in Gold Leaf Valley. Pamela is trying to kill us!"

Lauren's heart thudded in her chest as Pamela feinted toward her. She brandished the chair at the other woman.

She wasn't going to let Pamela hurt any of them!

"It's over, Pamela," she said breathlessly. "The police will be here any minute. You won't have time to kill all three of us before they arrive." Lauren certainly hoped that was true.

"But I can certainly try," Pamela snarled, charging toward Lauren.

Lauren shouted, meeting Pamela's attack with one of her own. She held the chair in front of her chest and face and lunged forward.

Pamela screamed and fell down at the same time a male voice commanded, "Police!"

"They tried to kill me," Pamela sobbed, curled in a ball on the floor and clutching her ankle. "They did it! They killed Steve."

Purrr. Purrr. Purrr." Annie growled the sound, her fur puffing up as she glared at Pamela.

Lauren was glad for Pamela's sake that Annie was still in her cat bed. She'd never seen the feline act like that before, but Annie obviously knew she and Zoe needed help.

"I think you'll find," Lauren told Mitch, slowly placing the chair on the floor with trembling hands, "that Pamela killed Steve." It was amazing that her voice sounded normal. She certainly didn't feel it.

"She confessed to us!" Zoe gestured at the weeping heap on the floor. "She stole belladonna from Mrs. Finch's garden."

"And I recorded it." Lauren motioned to the phone Zoe held.

"My ankle!" Pamela cried. "She broke it!" She pointed at Lauren.

"I saw the whole thing," Zoe said. "You must have hurt it when you fell over. Lauren's chair barely touched you, and it was total self-defense anyway!"

"Brrt!"

"It must be if Annie says so." Lauren laughed shakily and went over to her cat, picking her up and cuddling her. "Thank you," she whispered into Annie's furry neck.

Mitch cleared his throat.

"If you give me the recording, I'll bag it for evidence."

"Okay." Zoe handed over the phone. "We'll get it back, won't we?"

"Yeah," he replied. His gaze met Lauren's. "Are you okay to come to the station and make a statement?"

"Yes," she replied. "I want justice for Steve's death."

EPILOGUE

The next day, Lauren and Zoe were guilty of opening the café a little later than usual.

Lauren realized she hadn't been nervous when Mitch had appeared to take Pamela into custody, but that was understandable. There'd been too much going on at the time. Now, she wondered if the next time she saw him she'd still feel nervous – and attracted to him.

Pamela had been arrested for Steve's murder and was currently in jail awaiting trial. But with the recording of her confession, Lauren wondered if the middle-aged woman would decide to plead guilty.

"I can't believe what happened here yesterday." Zoe gestured to the vacant tables as they set up for the day.

"I know," Lauren said ruefully.

"Brrt!"

"I've never seen Annie look like that before when Pamela threatened us," Zoe continued thoughtfully, "or heard her purr like that."

"I looked it up last night," Lauren admitted. "Cats don't only purr when they're happy, they can also purr if they're afraid or about to go into battle."

"Annie certainly went into battle for us!" Zoe grinned at the Norwegian Forest Cat.

"Brrt!" Annie said proudly, perched in her cat bed.

A thought suddenly struck Lauren. "Annie, were you trying to help us find the killer when you showed us that Pamela left her black leather bag behind in the café that day?"

"Brrt!" Annie seemed to agree.

"That's right!" Zoe clapped a hand to her temple.

"We found out how close a neighbor Pamela was to Mrs. Finch when we returned her bag," Lauren said slowly. "And that's when the casino chip dropped out."

Zoe's eyes widened. "Annie, you helped solve the mystery!"

"Brrt!" Annie said proudly. "Brrt!"

"We'll have a lot to talk about with Mrs. Finch at knitting club on Friday night," Zoe said. "If I spend all my spare time until then I bet I can finish Annie's blanket."

"Please don't say that word." Lauren shuddered. "Bet."

"Sorry." Zoe looked contrite.

"We promised Mrs. Finch we'd bring Annie to knitting club this week. I'm so glad she's innocent."

"I know. Now we can totally enjoy her company without a faint niggle in the back of our mind wondering if she – you know."

"I know." Lauren nodded, then looked over at her cat. "Would you like to come to knitting club with us, Annie?"

"Brrt!"

"I know that's a yes!" Zoe grinned.

THE END

AUTHOR NOTE

Annie is based on my own Norwegian Forest Cat, who was also called Annie.

I hope you enjoyed reading this mystery. Sign up to my newsletter at www.JintyJames.com and be among the first to discover when my next book is published!

TITLES BY JINTY JAMES

Meow Means Murder – A Norwegian Forest Cat Café Cozy Mystery – Book 2

Spells and Spiced Latte - A Coffee Witch Cozy Mystery - Maddie Goodwell 1

Visions and Vanilla Cappuccino - A Coffee Witch Cozy Mystery - Maddie Goodwell 2

Magic and Mocha – A Coffee Witch Cozy Mystery – Maddie Goodwell 3

Enchantments and Espresso – A Coffee Witch Cozy Mystery – Maddie Goodwell 4

Familiars and French Roast - A Coffee Witch Cozy Mystery – Maddie Goodwell 5

Incantations and Iced Coffee – A Coffee Witch Cozy Mystery – Maddie Goodwell 6

Printed in Great Britain
by Amazon